MASTER
of
STARLIGHT

DW ARDERN

STALKING HORSE PRESS
SANTA FE, NEW MEXICO

PRAISE FOR DW ARDERN

"I fell in love with this book and happily under its spell on page one. Ardern is so clever, hilarious, and wise about how we survive the messes we make of our star-crossed lives in the name of love."
— Elissa Schappell, co-founder of Tin House
& author of *Use Me*

"*Master of Starlight* is a lush and consequential wonder, expanding and contracting with the energy of a universe twice its size. I loved it when I read it, and I carry it with me still, long after turning the last page."
— Ashley Warlick, author of *The Arrangement*

"In the Moroccan desert, a washed-up astronomer finds himself hosting his former friend and professional rival. What begins as an uneasy reunion spirals into a tense and morally fraught battle of ego, resentment, and desire. A fast-moving literary novel of ambition and heartbreak."
— Matthew Binder, author of *Pure Cosmos Club*

"A funny, poetic meditation on the points in life at which our orbits intersect."
— *Kirkus Reviews*

MASTER OF STARLIGHT
Copyright © 2025 by DW Ardern
ISBN: 978-1-960451-18-7

First paperback edition published by Stalking Horse Press,
November 2025

www.stalkinghorsepress.com

Design by James Reich
Chapter illustrations by Mikayla Sherfy

Stalking Horse Press
Santa Fe, New Mexico

MASTER of STARLIGHT

1.

RADIANT with starlight, galaxies and nebulas, quasars and clusters, the great fishbowl of infinity curved over the Sahara. The enigmatic universe and its boundless mysteries unfolded over the dunes like ribbons of silk, wide open in the fathoms of space above.

Every night, Olivier marveled at the stars from his outpost on the roof of the Porte d'Etoile hotel, revolving on planet Earth in orbit of its mother star, a solar thorn in the pinwheel of the Milky Way as the monstrous galaxy careened through the cosmos. Some nights, he would spend so long stargazing by the naked eye and the telescope's magnified refraction that he would forget whether he was right-side up or upside down.

He was a marveller by birth, by curiosity, by tutelage under his mentor the famed astronomer Wolfgang Hume, by wanderlust throughout his years of travel in South America, Africa, Asia, and the Pacific Islands. And now he had been a marveller by occupation for nine years as the resident astronomer of an oasis riad in the Tinfu Dunes of Morocco.

Olivier traced the Hercules constellation from Eta Herculis down toward its sister Zeta and located the foggy cluster of Messier 13. Grinding his sandals in the rooftop grit, he wrestled the huge cannon of his Celestron telescope toward an isolated patch of night sky. He looked in the viewfinder and made slight corrections. Almost on point. Almost perfect on first try. He took pleasure in small perfections. At 56 years old, it made him feel like his life wasn't such a lonely mess.

"Ah, there it is," he told the young couple waiting patiently for the next star. "This is Messier 13, a globular cluster in the constellation of Hercules 25,000 light years away."

His guests crowded the telescope. Olivier stepped away with a flourish, like a magician pleased by his illusion.

"It was named after Charles Messier, an ambitious eighteenth-century comet hunter who mistook every weird diffused object in the sky over Paris for a comet. He became famous for cataloguing each one, and oh-so-humbly granting them his surname."

His guests for the evening were tireless. The starry-eyed young woman with henna-rouged hair was an amateur astronomer, accustomed to silence in quiet admiration. Her somewhat dim-witted boyfriend was the one with a knack for asking irritating questions at the most inopportune moments, hands stuffed in his leather jacket, trying desperately to feign interest in celestial objects on such a frigid night.

From midnight till now, 3 a.m., with a few short hours till the desert rose of dawn, they'd traveled thousands of parsecs into the deep dark loneliness of space, gazing through the telescope lens at the lost light of history. He'd shown his guests the spiral disc of Andromeda, Saturn's rings, the bright double-vision blot of Albireo, swinging his telescope on a desultory journey through the constellations, the map of stars slated in perfect darkness by a new moon.

"In truth, M13 was first discovered by Sir Edmund Halley…"

"Is that the astrologer dude who discovered Halley's Comet?"

"Akk!" Olivier clutched his throat, choking on the insult. "Astronomy, young man. Not astrology. This is science. If you want me to read your tarot later, I can but I'm lousy at fortunes. I don't even believe in the future."

"What do you believe in then?"

"Probability, possibility… entropy, most of all. You will too someday."

The henna-haired stargazer chuckled and peered into the telescope. Her boyfriend shoved his fists deeper in his pockets.

"Where were we? Ah, yes, Edmund Halley was the first astronomer to predict the orbital cycle of what's now known as Halley's Comet. However, there have been records of that legendary cosmic spitball going back to Chinese astronomers during the Qin dynasty."

While his guests spied on the M13 cluster, Olivier hunted for his next coordinates in the gaseous band of the Milky Way flaming like a rocket tail through the pantheon of stars. Capella? Too obscure. Perhaps Neptune's asteroid belt and be done with it. He noted some faint clouds drifting in with their opaque scrim.

He let loose a pinch of sand. The wind was blowing east. Clouds were his worst enemy. Invisible at night except to the most discerning, the keenest eye.

He looked for Beta Lyrae—his obsession, his faithful friend, his counsel—known as Sheliak to the ancient Arabian astronomers. An eclipsing binary star in the constellation of Lyra, sometimes shy and sometimes brilliant, but always spirited. He found the curious star shining indigo like an oracle among its shimmering attendants. Sheliak dimmed and brightened, pulsing like a beating heart.

The henna-haired stargazer excitedly beckoned her boyfriend over to take a look at Messier 13.

Olivier flipped the collar on his denim jacket. He no longer disguised his shivering. His hands were tired, his mind wandered. He wanted to go to bed.

"Isn't it beautiful?" she said.

Yes, yes, it is, Olivier thought, in admiration of her ebullience at 3 a.m. in morning. She reminded him of Vera. Rebellious, galvanized by a sort of ecstatic beauty. Her childlike wonder, spellbound by the stars, her eyes cosmic and adrift in the mystery of time and space, like him, or like he once was before he lost her.

"There's nothing there… wait, no, it's gone." Her boyfriend fiddled with the focus ring. "The telescope is kind of wobbly. Maybe something's wrong with it?"

Olivier, with a not-so-discreet harrumph, waved the idiot off and looked into the eyepiece. Darkness. He adjusted the telescope 30mm south, then west, then east in case the careless young man had again moved it out of alignment with his shaky grip. He tracked down the dense cluster, its brilliant dynamo of yellow and blue light like confetti, the telescope uncooperative with an oddly stubborn heaviness. And then he lost it again, the instrument jiggling out of whack. He glanced under the broad metal cylinder, spying orange fur and claws toying with the chassis.

"Tiku! No, stop it. Get off of there."

Olivier shook the giant telescope as the scrawny kitten clung underneath refusing to let go. She finally tumbled off with a feral caterwaul and scurried out onto the rooftop—a tabby cat with patches of orange and white fur, her right ear flopped like a deflated balloon.

The henna-haired stargazer laughed. "Oh, she's adorable."

Tiku glanced up at them with fierce yellow eyes, perplexed by her offense. She raced under the astronomer's legs.

"Don't encourage her. She's nothing but a troublemaker." Olivier bent down and whistled softly. Tiku clawed her way up his jacket before seating herself triumphantly on his shoulder. He petted the shy kitten. "Well, that's all the show we have for tonight."

The stargazers thanked him. Olivier forced a smile and gestured, rubbing his forefinger and thumb. It took the stargazers a moment or two, gawking at the shaggy-haired astronomer and his furry companion, before they realized what he was doing.

"Are you serious? Fine." The boyfriend handed over a few dirham. "Thanks again."

"My pleasure," Olivier said, pocketing the coins. "A word of advice? Never ask a man if he's serious in the desert. The Sahara suffers no fools."

＊

THERE was once a time when Olivier believed he had a destiny, a modest but important fate mapped out in the stars. He'd devoted the self-assured clarity and insatiable curiosity of his youth to the movement of the stars, though not just their affixed position in the firmament as soulless navigation points that seafarers had relied on to explore the world and modern astronomers used to chart the visible universe.

He held the unshakable belief that the stars were more alive than presumed by conventional science. This belief had been forged from a lifelong intimacy with the night sky—from his childhood years in Belgium as a peculiar boy with thick spectacles who preferred to spend his time on the roof of his parents' house in De Hann rather than playing sjoelbak with the neighborhood boys, to his star-chasing adventures and nights of marvelous wonder peering out through telescopes in the farthest reaches of the world.

The stars are alive. They are born, they age, and they die. His goals were scientifically grounded. His thesis was scientifically grounded. He wanted to determine whether the stars' movements were willful or arbitrary. He reasoned that if we released ourselves from the vainglorious prejudice that consciousness was restricted to advanced organisms, that it was indeed a form of universal energy as the Jesuit philosopher Teilhard de Chardin had postulated, then it was only logical to assume that all elements of the cosmos were conscious at a base and reactive level, even the stars in their seemingly improvised mathematical beauty.

And what did he receive for his unorthodox beliefs among the celestial dreamers at the Sorbonne? Nothing but vitriol and ridicule. He was branded a heretic, an outsider, a kook. He was denied his PhD after failing to defend his thesis "The Ballet of the Stars" among the stodgy old men on the doctoral committee. Even Wolfgang Hume had been too cowardly to speak up on his behalf.

And so, he continued his studies elsewhere, freed from the shackles of academia. He'd dropped acid with the Berkleyites in 1975, communing with the stars on Telegraph Hill. He'd drunk kava with the Polynesians and heard their ancient stories about the birth of the earth and the heavens from the supreme Ta'aroa. He'd hiked Machu Picchu and learned the Incan cosmovision of Kawsay Pacha, prayed to Ch'aska Quyllur, the Venus star and goddess of dawn and twilight.

He'd stood on the ruins of the Alexandria library in Egypt, among its broken columns, knowledge burned and buried in centuries of dust, and thought of Eratosthenes, Hipparchus, Ptolemy, the mathematicians and stargazers of the ancient world, trying to solve empyrean mysteries. And during his travels in Morocco, where there were rocks older than stars, he'd met Karl Reinhardt, owner of the Port d'Etoile, watching Berber musicians dance with cymbals on their fingers at Dar Essalam in Marrakesh.

Maybe it was the plentiful Moroccan wine, but Karl didn't think Olivier's theories were outlandish. He was enamored with the astronomer's earnest passion for the stars.

He said: "Come to Tinfu. Continue your studies. You can be my resident astronomer."

It sounded like the call of destiny. It sounded like vindication, an opportunity to fully dedicate himself to investigating the inner life of the star. But after almost a decade in the desert, the Port d'Etoile felt more and more like the final prison of his exile.

*

THE soft-boiled egg was a harbinger of his imminent doom. For nine years, Olivier had eaten a single egg with a side of toast and a slice of melon for breakfast, alone in the sunny banquet room with its zellij-tiled floor and horseshoe arches open to the desert wind and dust. A hard-boiled egg, a special request that ran counter to Madame Habib's delicate soft-boiled eggs, but a simple request, nonetheless.

And now, after thousands of breakfasts and thousands of compliments to the chef and generous dirham tips, he pierced the fragile eggshell with his fingernail and the filmy bald embryo split, oozing its molten goo all over his melon.

Through the archway into the grand hall, he eyed Moussa with suspicion. The Maître d' of the hotel stood at his post behind the counter in the lobby, awaiting the morning's departures. Regal with his handsome Malian features, rigid with his humorless posture in a maroon uniform with a matching fez cap. Whenever Karl was away on business, Moussa and Olivier were left responsible for the daily operations of the riad. It was an awkward partnership. Moussa preferred the stately illusion that the Port d'Etoile was a historic hotel akin to the grand dames of Europe instead of a boring block of sandstone designed by a Japanese architect in the 1980s adorned with chintzy tin lanterns and threadbare rugs. He had little patience for astronomers and their ilk, including most of the riad's guests.

Moussa was always less than amused by Olivier's eccentric ways. The astronomer's unkempt hippie hair, the wiry untamed grey bush curling out from his ears. His denim jacket and ratty rock 'n' roll t-shirts, his baggy khaki shorts, sandals with socks. His inappropriate jokes with the guests, his cavalier attitude, his complete lack of decorum. Moussa tolerated Olivier in the same way one tolerates a stray dog that has somehow become the boss's pet. A feral and dangerous creature, a filthy animal that Moussa wished he could put out of its misery with a clean bullet to the head.

Olivier quarantined the unstable egg on a tea saucer. He wiped the goo off his melon and munched the slimy fruit. It was evident that their cold war of brusque civility and passive-aggressive smiles had expanded its boundaries. And now the treachery of a soft-boiled egg, its viscous tendrils spilling from the collapsed embryo. Somehow Moussa had courted Madame Habib to his favor. Olivier mashed the egg into a pulp with his fork.

Every day, the same monotony of hellfire sun, mundane chores, and dunescape purgatory at the Port d'Etoile. But it was worth it for the nights of perfect starlight, the twilight's prologue when the blue desert sky would vanish like a theater curtain whisked away for the greatest show on earth – the infinite universe, the interstellar playground of nebula, asteroids, stars, and planets. The rooftop was heaven on earth for the academic and amateur astronomers who made the pilgrimage through the Atlas Mountains and down the crumbled desert roads to the far end of the Draa Valley. They came from all over the world to be alone with the starlight and pure dark forever sky on an outpost in the sea of dunes. Which was all the more reason why Olivier felt like a fraud.

Olivier drank his black coffee. Absently, he drew nebulas and star clusters in the gooey yolk on his plate with his melon rind. He was tired of being treated like a child. Did you change the sheets? Did you check the water pressure in the shower? Did you set the air conditioner at 20°C? He was an astronomer, not a goddamn housekeeper. He was only supposed to greet the guests in Karl's absence and make sure they felt comfortable since he spoke seven languages and considerably better French and German than Moussa. He was positive that it had been Moussa's idea to install that infuriating bell in his room, so he couldn't sleep through any arrivals.

"Are you not hungry, Ollie?" Moussa had appeared at his shoulder, fingers gripped on the head of his chair.

"Sour stomach." Olivier continued his artistic rendering of the galaxy in yolk.

"Perhaps some mint tea?" He smirked. "Mr. Reinhardt says our special guests are scheduled to arrive by noon from Ouarzazate. I trust everything is prepared."

Olivier had been dreading the arrival of the special

guests. Fritz Konigsmann and his cavalcade of admirers, the prestigious German astronomer renowned for his work at the Leibniz Institute of Astrophysics. He knew Fritz from another life, when the dashing gentleman had been a pimple-poxed Düsseldork at the Sorbonne, when Olivier had been his classmate and closest friend, a waggish young scholar with aspirations as vast as the night sky. Fritz had booked out all seven rooms of the riad, a holiday at the edge of civilization so he could show off the immaculate desert stars to his colleagues. Or had his old friend secretly come back to see him and apologize? Doubtful. They were too alike in that regard, far too stubborn to ever relinquish their pride.

"Yes, the royal suite is ready for his highness," Olivier said.

Moussa's eyes drifted to a saucer of milk on a chair. He hunched down and found Tiku hiding under the table. "Hello, we haven't been supping at the table again, have we?"

The kitten scampered away through the sandstone arches, out into the courtyard.

"Madame Habib would not be happy about that." Moussa glowered. "Please make sure that little rascal is locked away by the time our guests arrive."

"Can't make any promises." Olivier sipped his coffee. "Tiku is a free spirit. She doesn't belong to me or anyone. She just sleeps in my bed."

"You misunderstand me," Moussa said. "There will be no funny business like the last time. She will behave. You will behave. This is very important. Konigsmann is bringing his wife."

His wife. Olivier downcast his eyes from the

inquisitor. He made broader strokes with the rind, spiraling out a black hole in yolk that obliterated his galactic doodle. Vera. So the rumors were true. It didn't matter. None of it mattered anymore.

"I thought Karl said she wasn't coming."

"Well, I guess plans have changed," he said. "Karl is anxious since we haven't had any real astronomers here in a long time. He wants to make sure they have an unforgettable experience."

"Am I not a real astronomer?" Olivier said.

"You don't want me to answer that question." Moussa pointed outside to the courtyard patio. "The Mendelsons have been waiting for you since 6 a.m. to see the sun. They were very disappointed they missed the sunrise."

Olivier glanced through the archway into the courtyard. The Mendelsons, polite Austrian orthodontists from Salzburg, were seated at one of the mosaic tables outside. They sipped their tea and forked their buttered crêpes, patient beside a solar telescope on a tripod.

"It's already set up," Olivier said. "It's not hard to find the sun."

"It is for our hospitality and expertise that people travel thousands of miles to come here." Moussa dismissed him with flick of his wrist and walked away.

Olivier damned Moussa under his breath, damned his fate in the dunescape limbo of the desert outpost. He refilled his coffee from the tin pot and went out to greet the Mendelsons.

✱

THE desert wind wheezed a shallow breath over the dunes through which an empty road slalomed, demarcated by cairns painted white and positioned like soldiers along the sinuous drive to the gates of the Port d'Etoile.

Olivier rolled a cigarette and smoked out the window of his room with a watchful eye on the long winding road through the dunes, waiting for a hot-sun chimera of rolling dust on the horizon. How long had it been since he'd seen her? Four years? Five years? Seasons passed in the desert with nothing to mark their passage beyond the arrival and departure of riad guests. Will I die here? he thought. Will I ever leave this place? What ultimately was the point of it all?

His studies had been abandoned long ago, his astrophysical theories on the personal life of the star. Dozens of journals, notebooks, binders of research stacked under his bed collecting dunes of dust. He'd tried for years to convince prestigious journals of the scientific validity of his beliefs, which was a hopeless endeavor without the proper credentials. And then Fritz, his old university pal with whom he'd had countless conversations on the subject, had published an acclaimed theory in Astronomy & Geophysics magazine on the peculiar behavior of binary star systems that borrowed greatly from his observations of Alpha Centauri, HD 98800, and of course the gravitational tango of Beta Lyrae.

He'd been angry at first, but Fritz, to his credit, had cited Olivier's contribution in the footnotes, so small he had to read it with a magnifying glass. He'd hoped this would give him an opportunity to finally publish some part of his life's work, even if it was only as a collegiate response to Fritz's theory. The rejection letters filled up a binder of their own.

These days, he reserved his opinions for private arguments with himself, reading the latest issue of Discover or Cosmos magazine. He spent his leisure time drinking canned beer in the privacy of his room, smoking and drawing the cat.

He puffed on his thin cigarette and read his horoscope in the morning newspaper. Another two-star day for Scorpio, an inauspicious moon in Sagittarius. Tiku sprawled on the windowsill in one of her glamor poses, dangerously close to plummeting off the ledge into the courtyard of palm trees and boulders. He sketched the kitten in the newspaper margins while savoring the last third of a Kostritzer tallboy, two days stale and flat. Conservation was key to survival in the desert. It was difficult to get any good sundries except figs, olives, nuts, and beans this far out in the Draa Valley. And so, whenever he traveled home to Belgium, he always smuggled an extra suitcase into Morocco stuffed with pretzels, chips, crackers, cans of tuna fish and tomato soup, a generous supply of Kostritzers, and the most coveted of all, pork sausages.

"Too much shadow, scooch." He gestured with his pencil. Tiku stretched her scrawny legs and repositioned herself, patches of orange fur ablaze with fiery lucence in the midday sun. Olivier shaded her deflated ear, sketched the furry curve of her arched back.

Sometimes, on moody days when a sullen nihilism would possess him, all romance for the desert lost, his good humor as scarce as rain in the Sahara, Olivier would sketch the black scorpion in the mason jar. The contours of its armor, its fat pincers like a boxer ready for a fight, its bulbous tail like a question mark curling out to the deadly thorn of its stinger. A grotesque little monster trapped in a glass prison on his bookshelf.

He'd found the venomous servant of death on the patio one sweltering afternoon last summer. He had taken a short walk in the nearby Tinfu Dunes and decided to enjoy a late lunch in the courtyard. He'd removed his boots and shook out the sand. The scorpion had surprised him while he was buttering his toast. He'd always imagined death would come for him like this. Sly and indifferent, slinking into his periphery. The scorpion skittered sideways, zigged, zagged across the stone tiles before hiding in the shadows of a large clay jug. They spied each other from afar. And then, as if challenging him to a duel, the scorpion crept toward his table, its stinger primed. Olivier leapt up and inched away. The scorpion skittered over the toe, up the leather tongue, and into his empty boot.

This was nothing new. He'd had many scares in the desert. He'd caught other scorpions before, sometimes inside the riad, delivering the deadly creature safely out into the dunes as if it were a harmless mouse or house spider. However, he'd never seen a black scorpion before. He tossed the flowers from a vase on the table and shook his boot out into the teardrop vessel. He was fascinated by the monster. He knew their legend from Egyptian, Persian, Arabian mythology. Ancient assassin. King killer. The famous Greek tale immortalized in the stars. Gaia's revenge upon the hunter Orion for threatening to kill all beasts on earth. So small and quiet, yet powerful enough to take down a demigod. And so Olivier kept it as trophy in a fat mason jar with a few pinholes in the lid, occasionally feeding it any beetles he'd find in his room, expecting the black scorpion would someday die on its own of old age.

Olivier smoked and drank warm beer. He added definition to the cat's sleepy eyes with his pencil. Still no sign of movement out on the dunes, no sound beyond the wind. He touched the medallion beneath his shirt, the cold yin-yang coin a salve against his hot skin. The bronze necklace had been a gift from a Taoist monk at a temple in Shanghai, intended to remind him of life's duality—the shadow and the light, ever changing. He treated it like a talisman, often tracing the yin-yang swirl with his index finger while mulling over an important decision, calculating possible outcomes, the most fortuitous path in the infinite multitude of paths. He sometimes asked it unanswerable questions, gazing up at the stars or sitting alone in his room.

"Does she love him?" he asked, rubbing the medallion. Tiku perked up on the windowsill with her good ear cocked. "Do you think she loves him?" The tabby cat licked her paws in the bright sunlight from the window. "You're right. Of course, she does."

The problem was he liked Fritz Konigsmann. It was hard not to like Fritz, even with his ostentatious persona and convoluted theories on supernovas and hypervelocity stars. As the head of astronomy at the Leibniz Institute, he was entitled to his eccentricities. He was a brilliant scientist and tech savant, personally modifying the most advanced telescopes to capture images from deep in the cosmos. He'd been awarded numerous medals, grants, and honors from the European Astronomical Society. He'd been knighted by the Queen of England for Christ's sake.

Fundamentally, Fritz hadn't changed much from the rowdy student he'd met so many years ago. An amicable and excitable astronomer with a magnetic zeal for science and a complex understanding of celestial machinations. This was part of the reason they had been such good friends during their time at the university and remained in touch for decades afterward. That is until he learned of his betrayal.

It was too much to think about. Olivier crumpled up his drawing and threw it in the waste bin. He fetched a tin of tuna fish from the fridge and shared his lunch with Tiku. He drank the last of his beer and fell asleep before noon.

2.

SPRING of 1975. It was a beautiful day in Paris and Olivier's meticulously calculated life had just spectacularly fallen apart. He was twenty-four years old, plucky and self-assured of his brilliance. The youngest graduate student ever at the Sorbonne's doctoral school for Astronomy and Astrophysics. Recipient of three scholarships, two grants, and a prime candidate for a prestigious Royal Astronomical Society fellowship for post-doctoral research at the University of Cambridge once he matriculated.

He'd opened the heavy oak doors of the boardroom on the third floor as a scholar of promise and limitless potential. Once inside, the committee dissected his 168-page dissertation on the irregular behavior of binary-star systems like they were butchering a cow. Every argument, every data set, every conclusion. False equivalence, insufficient data! Speculation, circular logic! Olivier, in turn, had dissected the mothballed codgers, seated in herringbone jackets and cardigans, attacking their musty accolades and discredited theories along with an assortment of weird foibles and physical oddities like Dr. Edward Beaumont's chalk licking habit or Dr. Alain Tremblay's terrifying neck mole.

Two hours later, he walked out of that boardroom as an academic orphan. A scholar in exile. A rebel without a clue what do with his life. He swiftly collected his belongings from his dorm room in the weathered blue suitcase with which he'd arrived at the Sorbonne as a quiet timorous undergrad. The son of an iron-jawed, steel-toed boatbuilder at the one of the oldest and greatest scholastic institutions in all of Europe. He packed up his beloved Criterion Dynascope and left the brass key in the door, cursing every crooked stair of the residence on his way out.

"Ollie! How'd it go?" Fritz called, rushing out after him. Olivier ignored his friend, hefting his suitcase and telescope down the residence's broad front steps. The strap broke. The suitcase tumbled the rest of the way before busting open on the cobblestones.

He gathered his clothes and shoved them back in. "They are myopic old fools already in their graves."

He sat down with his pocketknife and recounted what had happened while he fixed the suitcase, slicing the torn ends of the broken leather strap into strands so he could tie them off. Fritz sat beside him on the steps and generously listened. Olivier knew what he would say. A silver lining, no doubt. Some well-intentioned but ultimately patronizing advice. Fritz had never known failure. He'd never had to worry about scholarships. He had the privilege of affluent parents and a bank account that always retained its zeros. He had no understanding of the fear that his life was a house of cards that could collapse at a moment's notice.

"It's just one more semester," Fritz said. "I'll put in a good word with the dean. My father is close friends with him. You can revise your dissertation and try again."

"And what do I do in the meantime?" Olivier said. "I can't afford to live in Paris on my own."

"I can loan you some francs, Ollie," Fritz said.

Olivier tightened the knots and stood with his suitcase. "I'll be fine."

"You're making a mistake."

"I'll send you a postcard." Olivier waved him off, trudging with his cases through the campus gardens toward Avenue de André Rivoire.

*

OLIVIER may not have been the scion of a wealthy family, but he was extraordinarily clever. This was how he'd survived. His cleverness had saved him from snaggle-toothed bullies in the streets of De Hann. It had earned him top marks in the university with his ingenious systems for memorizing complex physics equations that confounded his peers. It had allowed him to camouflage his working-class roots with the professorial flair of a tweed jacket and flourished accent, taming his wild bushy hair with Brylcreem. All was not lost. He had the remainder of his scholarship money for the semester. He had some meager savings from working as barback at Les Deux Magots in the Latin Quarter. And perhaps his most precious asset, he had the solid-gold audacity of youth.

That night, he slept under the stars down on the Siene riverwalk near Pont des Invalides. Laid out on his jacket, resting his weary head on a sweater stuffed with socks for a pillow, he regretted his rash decision to vacate his dorm without a decent night's rest. The fairy-dust brilliance of Messier's jewels over the 7th arrondissement was a consolation that made the damp limestone and curious rats tolerable. It was the right decision, he assured himself. Earlier, on a bench with his cases inside the Gare du Nord station, he had for a split second—or rather an hour and half, eating an overly mustardy ham-and-cheese baguette sandwich—considered going home to Belgium. His parents were so fawningly proud of his accomplishments. The first generation of his family to attend university, let alone pursue a doctorate. This was his burden. His problem to solve. Under the stars with a million points of light for guidance, he felt something akin to revelation. For once in his young life, he was free to do whatever he wished. And that was intoxicating.

The next day, he took an overnight train to Barcelona where he had a few friends and a fair-weather lover—a dancer, painter, and free spirit—he'd met on holiday. After a couple nights of forgetting his epic failure at the Spanish discos and a couple more days laying gut-sick in his lover's apartment recovering from the recovery, he phoned his American friend Dexter from his undergraduate days at the Sorbonne.

Dexter, a proud Black scholar and unapologetic Marxist, had always been reliable counsel with his novel points of view, which he'd expounded at length—solicited or not—at the Latin Quarter cafes with other university students. They'd spent whole afternoons over café au lait and cigarettes, debating philosophy, science, physics, metaphysics, sociology, and of course politics. It had been Dexter who turned him onto the mid-century French philosophers—Pierre Teilhard de Chardin, Jacque Derrida, Maurice Merleau-Ponty, Michel Foucault—which had challenged his perspectives on consciousness, free will, and society at large. Sadly, in his third year, Dexter had been expelled from the Sorbonne and subsequently deported for what they deemed "unsavory behavior befitting a scholar" for the minor infraction of organizing the armed occupation at the Nanterre campus and later giddily throwing Molotov cocktails at riot police during the May Day protests. He was now teaching anthropology at the University of Berkeley in the bay area of San Francisco. Dexter was delighted to hear of Olivier's rebellion and badgered him until he relented.

And so, with only a few thousand francs in his bank account, Olivier bought a one-way plane ticket to the fabled city of beatniks, hippie cults, and flowers. Looking out the porthole window, he felt like winged Mercury soaring through the clouds, over the Atlantic Ocean, the majestic scope of America's continental expanse morphing from wetlands and rivers to cities, mountains, forests, miles and miles of farmland. The land of opportunity, innovation, revolution.

"You're free, Ollie," Dexter told him at a jazz club in the Tenderloin. "Do you know how lucky you are? No obligations, no iron club of the institution ready to knock you upside the head if you step out of line."

It wasn't hard to fall in love with San Francisco.

Its charmed hills of pastel Victorians. Its cable cars, neon bars, bookshops. Rebel hair, denim jackets, bell-bottoms. A fairytale city of magnolia and wisteria cast in a nostalgic dreamlike fog. It felt like the afterlife.

"This city makes me want to be a poet," Olivier said.

"You can be anything you dream here," Dexter said. "I'm thrilled for your reinvention."

Dexter and his friends were a shaggy bunch of intellectuals, much different than his pinched-spectacled colleagues at the doctoral school for Astronomy and Astrophysics. They were self-proclaimed revolutionaries. A professor of radical economics, an underground journalist, a funk musician. Dexter's girlfriend, with a gorgeous afro and bullet sash, was an avowed Black Panther, a group with which Dexter was not-so-secretly involved. They spoke of Malcolm X, tricky Dick Nixon, Vietnam, the fall of Saigon, the military industrial complex, the necessity and inevitability of a socialist revolution to liberate the working class and hopefully save the planet from a neo-feudalist imperial agenda. Their monologues were as ecstatic and percussive as the runaway jazz from the trio in the smoky club.

Everyone around the booth, its torn red leather peppered with cigarette burns, was genuinely interested in astronomy and well-versed in the latest discoveries. Public enthusiasm for space exploration was at an all-time high, thanks to the Apollo missions, the Soviet probe of Venus, Carl Sagan's elegiac history of the cosmos, and of course a very popular TV show where dauntless cosmonauts explored hostile planets in spandex onesies.

Passing a joint around the booth, Dexter and his friends asked theosophical questions about the mysteries of time, space, matter, and the pinball wizardry of the cosmic arcade. What were his thoughts on the Big Bang? Was there life on Mars? What did it all mean? Theorical and rhetorical questions, as ethereal and insubstantial as the smoke that tangled from their cigarettes.

"The universe is a jester, playing pranks and posing questions that can never be answered," Olivier said. "I kind of like it that way."

"Sometimes the answers aren't out there… they're in here," Dexter said, tapping on his temple. He whispered to his girlfriend. She pulled out a small tin from her leather jacket and unclasped it. There were paper tabs inside with tiny purple microdots. She instructed him to stick out his tongue.

"What is it?" Olivier asked.

"Pure starlight," she said.

*

AROUND midnight, they stumbled out of the club and made the arduous climb up Telegraph Hill to meet with Dexter's friend Pascal. He was a fellow Berkeley professor who split his time between the Bay Area and Los Angeles where he was an astronomer at the Mount Wilson Observatory in the Pasadena hills. Lying on blankets, staring up at the melting starlight with their eyes and minds wide open, Pascal entreated the intellectuals to his personal tour through the night sky over the bay with an elegant Unitron telescope. Olivier and Pascal became fast friends, like a couple of nerdy kids obsessed with the same comics, the same oddly named superheroes—Kepler, Cannon, Einstein, Hubble. Even after half the gang of shaggy intellectuals had fallen asleep, star-gone on the lawn, Pascal and Olivier traded the Unitron back and forth, showing off their favorite celestial misfits with commentary on their significance.

Olivier told him what had happened at the Sorbonne, positing the destruction of his academic career as a willful rebellion instead of a swift unceremonious punt out the door. Pascal listened with interest to his theories on binary star systems.

"Albireo, Castor, Eta Aquilae of course…"

"Any stars in NQ4?" Pascal asked. "Beta Lyrae?"

"What's that?"

"A star system in the bottom lateral of the Lyra constellation," Pascal angled the telescope, hunting the night sky. "The ancient astronomers called it Sheliak, the harp."

Olivier told him that he'd heard of it. "It's near the Ring Nebula, yes?"

"That's the one, due west of the egg."

Pascal located the star and invited Olivier to take a look. Maybe it was the vast California sky or the three gin cocktails and fuzzy magic of the microdot tab. Whatever the reason, seeing the dazzling twin star for the first time, Olivier was stunned by its serenity, as if he were witnessing some enigmatic truth in its hypnotic dance. He spent several minutes observing it. He was, in short, in love.

He removed his eye from the telescope. "It's wonderful."

"I know," Pascal said. "You should see it from Mount Wilson."

*

OLIVIER had only intended on staying a week at Mount Wilson, a long drive down California's golden coast to Los Angeles and the Pasadena hills. Riding along Pacific 1 with its jutting cliffs like an Olympian castle on the sea, he had the feeling that this was the start of a great adventure, liberated from his cosseted scholastic life to seek a destiny of his own in the great wild world.

He would learn to trust these feelings, this sort of uncanny intuition, what he would later consider—after decades of meditation, New Age philosophy, and recreational drug use—the calling of the Tao. Moments of sudden elation and total calm, vibrations through his whole being, when time would resonate like a bell in a tower, possible futures rippling out before him like waves from a single point of origin. At the Sorbonne, he'd been trained to repress his daydreaming nature, especially during his undergraduate studies. He'd minored in mechanical engineering, a practical science his father had pressured him into studying in case "the astronomy hobby" didn't work out. He became a conductor of experiments. Apostle of the empirical. Logic and reason. Every action governed by kinetic forces. Every consequence predictable. Out in the sunny freedom of California, he rediscovered the spirit that originally had drawn him into the night sky. A mysterious, amorphous part of himself. The dreamer, flowing with the waves, vigilant of the tides.

Shortly after his arrival at Mount Wilson, Olivier began conspiring to stay. He was rivetted by the observatory's extraordinary optical power from the first time Pascal showed him the Hooker telescope, which had famously delivered Edwin Hubble many of his greatest discoveries. During the day, Olivier aided Pascal in his administrative duties. After work, they'd sit out in the hills, smoke pot, and talk about wormholes, lightspeed travel, and the possibility of extraterrestrial life somewhere out there in a galaxy far, far away. Late at night, Olivier would sneak out from the guest quarters—what the team fondly called the Monastery—and employ the telescope to study his growing catalogue of curious binary star systems, especially Sheliak. He'd watch the harp dance for hours, Beta Lyrae A and B trading energy and mass in orbit.

Coincidence or fortunate probability, Mount Wilson had acquired a federal grant to modernize the observatory. Olivier made friends with the engineers on the project, who were annoyed at first by this rambunctious little man who wouldn't stop talking. He shadowed the engineers' work and asked them endless questions, which seemed naïve until they led to solutions. His spirited ingenuity and remarkable foresight to predict problems before they occurred soon charmed the engineers who started calling him "Ollie the Oracle."

The only person not charmed was Dr. George Welkins, the oldest member of the team and lead project manager. At 70 years old, he was suspicious of the free-loving hippie youth in general and especially wary of this brash young man who delighted in making sexual innuendos about the Hooker telescope and its protracting mechanisms.

One afternoon, on the observatory floor, when he'd had enough of Olivier's antics, Dr. Welkins challenged him to name the four key components of the new data relay, a near impossible task since most the engineers hardly knew how it worked. The mainframe computer and linked consoles had come directly from NASA's White Sands Laboratory. Olivier stalled, flustered, stuttered. It was a humiliation he would not soon forget.

After two weeks at Mount Wilson, with less than a hundred dollars left to his name, Olivier insinuated, perhaps not too subtly, that he'd be willing to stay and help with the project if Pascal would sponsor a working visa.

"I'm afraid that's not possible," Pascal said. "I wish it was."

"You're the boss," Olivier chided him. "You can send this Belgian dog with his tail tucked between his legs back to Europe if it doesn't work out."

"Dr. Welkins has autonomy over that team."

"He's a forgetful old man. You're going to trust him? What if something goes wrong?"

"He's been here longer than I have, Ollie. We're a family. It wouldn't be right."

The solution to Olivier's dilemma presented itself one day after lunch. He was finishing a peanut butter and jelly sandwich—entirely unimpressed by the gooey white bread and strawberry jam that tasted like chemicals—when he noticed some papers on the kitchen table. On closer inspection, he saw that it was the list of materials for the telescope's new cradle, accidentally left behind by Dr. Welkins. His nerves electrified. Time suspended with a strange resonance. A bell tolling in a tower. A sign from the universe. He could feel it. The list written on a yellow legal pad, a sharpened pencil beside it. What were the chances? he thought. What was the probability that he would be here at this precise moment to push luck toward his favor? And so, Olivier discreetly changed the measurements of all the interlocking joints, cylinders, pistons, cables, and wires on the list by a single decibel.

A week later, Dr. Welkins was forced into early retirement when the engineers attempted to assemble their painstaking design like children fussing over puzzle pieces that didn't quite fit. Olivier was hired as interim project manager to avoid any further delay in the construction.

It was a natural role for Olivier, even though he looked like a buffoon in his madras shirts and corduroy pants, his oval spectacles and bushy curls. However, he quickly earned the team's respect with his unique way of thinking—how he could work with his own hands and think through others. Troubleshooting mechanics, optical alignment, data output. Nearing the end of his six-month visa, a visiting astronomer told him about a new telescope at the University of the Philippines and their need for the expertise of a French-speaking project manager versed in astrometry and mechanical engineering.

In Manilla, he further proved himself as an ingenue, shepherding one of the largest telescope installations in the Pacific Islands. He was admittedly a lousy project manager, frequently napping on the job, blaring Neil

Young & Crazy Horse from his 8-track boombox, and often reeking of marijuana, but his scrappy reputation, foresight, and resourcefulness set him apart from the eggheads. Armed with his cleverness, he could take one glance at a schematic after hearing an engineer's issues and present multiple possible solutions.

So began his free-wheeling life as an itinerant astronomer. He traveled the world, hopping from project to project, overseeing observatory repairs, upgrades, and installations. Nobody pressed the question about his credentials. When asked, he would simply tell them he'd earned his doctorate from the Sorbonne. Before he knew it, seven years had passed. Although he made many friends and occasional lovers during his travels, he had no home beyond a boathouse in the Bruges harbor where he kept his books. He had no anchor in his life. Until that fateful trip in Bolivia that led him to a rebellious astrophysicist with stars in her eyes who would change everything.

3.

COME nightfall, the Port d'Etoile was spellbound by the magic of candlelight and a lion roar of infectious laughter. A boisterous jubliant energy reverberated from the special guests milling about the grand hall and parlor rooms. Fritz Konigsmann and his entourage—seven colleagues from the Leibniz Institute, all famous astronomers in their own right, and his wife Vera Durer, the lone astrophysicist in the group. The vaulted rooms had been enchanted with a generous decoration of throw pillows and colorful rugs, candles and incense, ornate lanterns of gilded stained-glass that hung low from the rafters casting mesmeric patterns of light and shadow. The seductive charms of Morocco. A sultan's opulence of firelight, shiny trinkets, and golden thread.

Everyone was in a celebratory mood with the exception of the canaries twittering in their cages. The poor birds had given up trying to sleep, as had Olivier who came downstairs, bleary-eyed and disheveled from his nap.

The special guests had arrived in the late afternoon, a storm of dust rolling down the desert road, three 4x4s and an RV with a giant blue telescope ratchet-strapped to the roof. Karl, Moussa, and Madame Habib were waiting with traditional mint tea and silver platters piled high with pistachio and fig-filled cookies. Olivier had slept through their arrival, ignoring the ringing bell in his room for three hours until the raucous merriment downstairs forced him out of bed.

He joined the welcome party and gulped down a glass of champagne just in time to be pulled aside by Karl and receive a not-so-subtle lecture about his tardiness. Olivier gave his apologies and said his stomach had gone sour over breakfast. A spoiled egg, soft-boiled he pointedly noted, was most likely the culprit. The farce of his contrition was thankfully interrupted by Fritz who'd spotted him from the courtyard.

"Ollie! You old dog, come here," he called out.

Fritz looked decades older, even though it had only been a couple years since they'd last seen each other, when he'd made a similar trip with some British astronomers after visiting the Oukaïmeden Observatory in the Atlas Mountains. He seemed almost frail now, gangly and near bald, his once wavy hair thinned and parted by a broad landing strip, distinguished wrinkles carved in his forehead from academic consternation. Olivier found comfort and renewed kinship in their mutual mortality. The shadow of death and time added a new dimension of humility to his showmanship.

"So good to see you, my friend," Fritz said. "You look like you just crawled out of a dune."

"I'm not feeling well," Olivier said.

"That's a shame. You'll be joining us for dinner though, won't you?"

Olivier had established his excuse. He'd planned to just say hello and return to his room so he could hide under the covers. It wasn't a total lie. His stomach was twisted, his chest so tight that he could hardly breathe. Across the banquet room, Vera chatted with a young German astronomer, her blonde hair silver streaked. She shimmered like a mirage in the lantern light, a coupe glass in her hand, elegant and confident in a pale yellow blouse and white linen slacks with a gemstone-studded belt.

Olivier wanted to make his apologies and bow out for the evening. However, the gleam of childish joy in Fritz's blue eyes was something he could never refuse. Olivier said he'd be honored and let his old friend lead him through the party like the prize pony at the county fair.

*

THE Port d'Etoile's resident astronomer. That's how Olivier was introduced. That was his illustrious title. Nothing short of embarrassing when compared to the special guests of the evening. There was Gustav Von Bokenbrink, who'd discovered sixteen exoplanets in the search for a second earth. Hugo Lavigne, esteemed cartographer of radioactive noise. Ingrid Leibenger, chief engineer in charge of the Spitzer Space Telescope. Allister Yahnel, comet and asteroid specialist.

At dinner, Olivier sat next to Saul Muller, a quiet and unassuming Canadian who'd won the Shaw Prize for his evidence on the extraordinary gravitational pull of blackholes. Olivier listened passively to Muller's explanation of his work, distracted by the jibes and heated discussions at the table about dark energy, relative motion of periodic orbits, and a massive new optical telescope at the South African Astronomical Observatory in Karoo.

Across the long table, over the cornucopia of fresh fruit, clay bowls of salted almonds and olives, plates of pigeon pastille, Vera picked from a mound of dates. She smiled warmly in the candle's lambent flicker. It felt almost romantic, the way she looked at him, the way she searched for his eyes over the apricots and oranges, the way she mouthed "How are you, Ollie?" inaudible amid the chatter at the table. It would have been romantic if it weren't for how her thin fingers were entwined with Fritz's hairy hands, their silver wedding bands casting glints of candlelight.

"The discovery of Gliese 581c has profound implications for the continued investigation of habitable exoplanets in that system…"

"There's no doubt about that, Fritz," Gustav said. "But it would be prudent for the scientific community to once, just once, reserve judgment before extrapolating speculative theories based on nothing but preliminary data…"

"Always a pragmatist, Gustav!" Fritz said. "That excitement is exactly what we need to get people invested in space exploration again. They should know the names of the great contemporary astronomers… the modern day Galileos, such as our own Ingrid Leibenger."

"You're too kind, Fritz," Ingrid said. "I'd personally rather stay anonymous. I'll take grant money over fame any day of the week."

"That's exactly the problem, isn't it? We're not monks. We're scientists. We must shake off our doubts and anxieties. We must be bold and assertive, come out of the comfy hermitages in our observatories so we can champion our discoveries."

"What's the point?" Allister said. "Wasted effort, if you ask me."

"The ignorance of the public is our own damn fault, that's my point. Over the past decade, we've made more progress in understanding the universe than in the past fifty years combined. And who knows this? Why is it still a battle to fund our research?" Fritz said, topping off his glass. "This is our challenge. We must broaden their curiosity beyond earth into the great unknown, make them understand that we are living on a mere dust mote twirling in eternity, a tiny blue marvel in a solar system among billions in our own galaxy, not to mention the countless galaxies scattered across the observable universe. Wouldn't you agree, Ollie?"

Olivier plucked an olive pit from his mouth and wiped off his fingers on a napkin. "If it is possible. I don't have much hope. The inward obsession of this new generation has engulfed any desire for a greater comprehension of the cosmos. They're not interested in anything other than themselves. The sun rises and falls for every idiot in their own mind."

"Ha!" Fritz said. "You jest, but I've known you long enough to know your cynicism for what it is."

"And what's that?" Olivier asked.

"Modesty, disappointment, frustration," Fritz said. "You discount the importance of what you do here. Every night, you show people the majesty of our vast elegant universe. This is what we all must do. We must move beyond lecturing the academic elites, excite the general public and reignite their sense of wonder in the stars."

Olivier drank his champagne, touched by these kind words. The feeling was short-lived, overshadowed by a deep guilt, the queasy nervousness he felt whenever he happened to catch Vera's sun-fire eyes across the table. Moussa whispered in Karl's ear, never lurking far from the dinner table with his arms crossed at attention behind his back.

"Splendid, yes," Karl told him.

Moussa snapped his fingers and out from the curtain came Madame Habib and her helpers from the kitchen. They cleared away enough space for the tagines and removed the tops, steam clouds rising with spice and sweetness. The guests sweated in the heat from the stewed lamb, chicken, and goat sizzling in olives, onions, carrots, and dates.

"This is the most traditional of Moroccan dishes," Karl said. "The delightful tagine. Enjoy."

The smell was overbearing. Olivier hated tagines. Overcooked vegetables and sweet meat simmered in ras el hanout. Once a month, maybe, he could stomach a tagine, a dish so revered as the culinary jewel of Moroccan cuisine that it was impossible to refuse without insulting the chef, host, and proud citizens of the country all at once.

Olivier waited for the guests to scoop their fill and

sear their tongues before he ladled out a hunk of lamb and some vegetables, merely out of courtesy, worried that Madame Habib might be observing from afar.

Vera crinkled her nose in silent revulsion. All her childhood friends stewed in spices. She'd been raised on a farm in the Netherlands and rarely ate meat. Olivier remembered when she'd confessed this during their first supper together as likeminded travelers, as soon-to-be friends, camping out under the blanket of stars on the salt flats in Bolivia. "Even chicken?" he'd asked. She touched her heart and said, "Oh dear god, no. I could never. Some of my first friends were chickens. I only eat pork. Pigs are disgusting animals."

Twenty-five years ago, Olivier thought as he tore bread and scooped up the mush of onions and carrots. After their serendipitous meeting in the salt flats, they had traveled together for three weeks exploring the wild countryside of Patagonia. He fell in love with Vera the moment she waved goodbye from Punta Arenas, dwarfed and saddled down by her huge backpack. It was a heartbreak he hadn't anticipated. He'd spent so many years alone, convincing himself that he didn't need anyone, that his only love was the infinite cosmos.

Twenty-five years ago, Olivier thought as he poured himself another glass of champagne and passed a bowl of candied nuts across the table to Allister. Their stargazing adventures to the ends of the earth, letters, phone calls, friendly visits to see each other on holiday, his boathouse in Bruges and her farmhouse in Aalsmeer. A romance without even a single kiss.

And why? Had the moment never arisen? Had he always been too afraid?

When she finished her doctorate at Oxford, she'd called Olivier and asked him if he knew of any research opportunities in mainland Europe. He was already in Morocco, visiting the magical blue city of Chefchaouen. "Come here, it's gorgeous," he'd told her. She laughed over the phone. He recommended that she call his old friend Fritz in Berlin.

"Olivier, where did you study astronomy?" Saul asked, an idle attempt at chitchat with a mouthful of goat.

There was only one person at the table who knew his secret. Even Karl didn't know, thanks to the clever forgery framed in his bedroom. The addendum to his title, PhD ABD... All But Doomed to the desert.

"Olivier and I were colleagues at the Sorbonne," Fritz intervened on his behalf. "I owe the genesis of my theories on dark matter's effect on binary stars to his genius. The best stargazer in our class. What was that clunky old telescope you used to have?"

"A Criterion Dynascope," Olivier said.

"That's right! Marvelous little spyglass," Fritz said. "Olivier knew the night sky over the Seine by heart. The master of starlight."

The affectionate nickname was uttered in earnest, though it felt like a schoolyard tease. A reminder of their past, a poetic moniker that Fritz had invented for him during their university days.

Fritz drank the last sweet sips of his champagne. "Do you think we could persuade you to treat us to a midnight stargaze on the roof?"

✳

THE buoyancy of half a dozen bottles of champagne and the promise of a perfect starlit night carried the astronomers up the terraced stone steps to the rooftop. Their eyes widened under the brilliant black sea of light, children once again awestruck by its incomprehensible beauty, humbled by an existential diminution.

This was the master of starlight's domain. Olivier prepped four of the telescopes for his guests. The Celestron, Takahashi FSQ, Newtonian Astrograph, Stellarvue SVX. He ignored the giant blue phallus of the Voyager SX31 that Fritz had already unpacked and assembled on the roof.

Olivier tilted the telescopes skyward and targeted obscure highlights—pulsars, neutron stars, the moons of Uranus. His speed and accuracy were astounding. The astronomers watched in amazement at his deft skill and expertise in isolating these gems of deep space, without the guidance of GPS coordinates or computerized triangulation or any of the modern gadgets employed to conduct their celestial investigations. The astronomers clustered around the telescopes, delighted by what they saw. The naked universe. Not a digital facsimile or LCD image on a monitor. True starlight from thousands of light years away.

"Can you see Lacertae from here?" Ingrid asked.

"See the tail of the Lizard? It's there." He pointed. "Due west, very faint."

Olivier felt euphoric, floating away with the stars and the pride of his work, until he turned and caught sight of them. Fritz and Vera were leaning against the sandstone rampart. A secret kiss in the night shadow of the parapet. The kind of private romantic moment that no one would have noticed had they not been looking for it.

Olivier flipped his jacket collar. There was a drift of cloud cover coming from the northwest. He let loose a pinch of sand. No such luck. The wind was moving eastward. They had thirty minutes at most before the sky was marred by clouds.

"Ah, a Kreutz comet!" Fritz exclaimed. "Did you see that, Ollie?"

"Or maybe it was one of your runaway stars?" Olivier said.

"Hypervelocity stars," Fritz corrected him. "The question I've yet to answer is what are they running away from." He gazed out from the ramparts at the immense starlight of the desert. "I'm in love with this place, Ollie. I must admit I'm jealous of your stars. You should come to Germany sometime. The Leibniz Institute has a fabulous observatory. I'm very lucky."

"Yes, you are," Ollie said, looking over his shoulder at Vera who was helping Saul angle the Stellarvue SVX toward some unknown prize in the night sky. "Maybe I'll come to Europe if there's some special occasion? A wedding perhaps?"

"You're mad that we didn't invite you to the ceremony. That's fair," Fritz said. "After what happened on my last visit, I didn't think you'd be interested."

"You didn't ask."

"You wouldn't return my calls. What the hell was I supposed to do?"

"It doesn't matter, Fritz. I'm happy for you."

Olivier walked away and helped Gustav locate the Pleiades and the dazzling meteoroids of the Seven Sisters.

He busied himself answering questions and locating galactic anomalies in the sky for the astronomers. He distracted himself from his grumbling stomach, the deep plunge of his heart, a sudden submission to gravity. A rocket's return to the atmosphere from orbit.

The night clouds moved in swift and obscured the sky with faint streaks of grey illuminated by a sliver of moonlight. He slowed his gait between telescopes until the stars were all but lost behind the phantom clouds. He told the guests that they would have to wait it out, an hour perhaps.

A loud whine disrupted the silence, a motor whir and cranking of gears. Fritz was priming the Voyager SX31. He configured the settings and punched in coordinates. The gigantic telescope rotated its cylinder and protracted a massive lens.

"A few pesky clouds are no match for the Voyager SX31," Fritz said. "Take a look at M42."

The astronomers gathered round the monstrous Voyager, its digital monitor so bright it was blinding in the dark. On the screen, in full color and crisp high definition, the purple and orange gaseous swirls of the Orion nebula. Olivier was soon abandoned among his refractor telescopes.

He'd had enough of Fritz's bravado for one night. He'd decided to shuffle off to bed when he felt a light touch on his arm.

"How have you been, Ollie?" she asked.

His first instinct was to remain armored, hold fast to his stoicism, meet her warmth with cold indifference. But he could never stay mad at Vera, the way she looked at him with those supernova eyes. What color were they? A dazzling cosmos unto itself of bright green, sky blue, nebulous ocher, solar flares of yellow.

"I'm fine. Thwarted by clouds once again," he said. "Did you get my letter?"

"Yes, it was very sweet." She hugged him. "Oh, Ollie. I've missed you."

She held him so close and so long he could feel her heart beat against his chest. A familiar rhythm as their hearts slowed and synced, followed by rumbles from both their stomachs.

"You hungry?" Olivier asked.

"Starving," she said.

"Me too," Olivier said. "If you're interested in a late-night snack, I have some contraband sausages in my room."

"Tempting," she said, glancing up at the clouded stars. "Alright, sure. Let's go before Fritz starts another one of his lectures."

4.

FALL of 1982. After another itinerant year of chasing stars and international projects, Olivier returned to his boathouse in Bruges, troubled by the quicksand of his waning youth. He was, by all accounts, an accomplished man—he'd traveled the world three times over and collaborated with some of the greatest minds to ever grace an observatory. However, he couldn't shake the sinking feeling that he'd somehow become his father's son—a builder, a mechanic, a facilitator of other's visions while his own languished, unseen and unrecognized. Regardless, he enjoyed his scruffy reputation as an iconoclast with radical theories on the metaphysical nature of the stars. His travels throughout Asia and the Middle East had only furthered his convictions, fascinated by the mysticism of ancient China, Persia, India, which posed important questions about energy, consciousness, and the transience of the material world.

He was indeed a scientist caught between East

and West, which he discovered much to his displeasure when, on his return from a month-long project at the University of Shanghai, he was detained in London for three days under the suspicion of being a communist spy and double agent. He took comfort that there was a sea change on the horizon—the burgeoning field of quantum mechanics, which challenged the veracity of Newtonian empiricism and aligned with his own cosmic views, and the fact that the Space Race had begun to thaw the Cold War, the apocalyptic chess game tactically shifting from bombs and spy planes to thermal rockets and spacecraft.

Later that fall, Olivier traveled on a diplomatic mission with a consortium of international scientists to the Pulkovo Observatory in St. Petersburg. Although it was never explicitly stated, he suspected his invitation from the Société Astronomique was a test to prove his loyalty and suss out whether or not he was communist spy. Afterhours at the French Consulate General, the scientists traded shots of vodka and made patriotic declarations affirming the West's entrepreneurial spirit as crucial to the arguably socialist pursuit of expanding humanity's comprehension of the universe. Recent advancements in radioastronomy had fueled urgency to upgrade the '60s-era optical telescopes throughout the world including South America.

Olivier remained silent on his own political views. He was grateful, however, that the Soviets and Americans seemed more intent on exploring other planets than an idiotic war that could obliterated all life on our own. He made grand statements about the West's scientific prowess and talked his way into joining the team at Cerro Tololo Observatory in Chile where an array of deep-space telescopes had been planned on behalf of the Americans.

The project lasted over two years in the Atacama Desert. It was one of the most complicated and ambitious jobs of his career. He helped the engineers and computer scientists develop a series of infrared and radio telescopes that could transmit observation data directly to the Carnegie Institution of Science via a satellite-linked network known as ARPANET. He was fascinated by this interstellar game of catch—capturing information from the stars, packaging it into code, and then pinging it back into outer space so it could be relayed down to someplace halfway around the globe.

Shortly before his 32nd birthday, Olivier finished his assignment at Cerro Tololo. He decided to make a solo excursion to Bolivia where he'd been told that the starlight's reflection on the salt flats was something beyond imagination. He left at sunrise and drove a rusty orange Chevy Chevette north through the Atacama Desert, crossing the border into Bolivia. It was night by the time he arrived at Salar de Uyuni, the scrubby earth smoothing out onto a giant wet frontier of salt. He'd been warned that it was dangerous to drive too far onto the flats at night, but he would not be deterred. He drove another 20 kilometers into the middle of the shining white heart enshrined by the majestic Andes. He parked near Isla del Pescado, one of the rocky cactus-spiked outcroppings that served as landmarks in the salt flats. He marched, determined, ladened with his telescope case and rucksack, the night sky perfectly mirrored on the salt as if he were traversing the Milky Way on foot.

He had come to see the Southern Hemisphere's Omega Centauri in all its glory and observe the behavior of certain binary systems in the globular cluster. He'd mapped out the GPS coordinates for the relative center of Salar de Uyuni. He would settle for nothing less than the perfect outpost for his observations.

Trekking out onto the flats, he was perturbed to hear a transistor radio playing American folk music. The music grew in volume. It was coming from precisely where he was headed. He could see the vague outline of a jeep stationed out on the salt. He walked toward the song as the sweet voice of Joni Mitchell wavered over the flats, deeply annoyed that his birthday stargazing trip was being ruined by a tourist. He crept closer, passing the jeep. A chair, propane stove, sleeping bag. The angular jut of a telescope, its owner nowhere to be seen. It was one of the new portable Celestrons. He peeked in the viewfinder. It was focused on Omega Centauri.

"Hello? Can I help you? That's mine."

He looked over his shoulder, surprised to discover a young woman standing there out on the flats, her blonde hair tied in a ponytail, her overalls covered in salt. Later, for years, Olivier would often replay this moment over and over in his mind, trying to make sense of its magic. Was it circumstance? Was it fate? Her eyes struck him with their cosmic fire. He was captivated by this mysterious woman who'd surfaced from the salty darkness. He interpreted her intensity as an undeniable magnetism between them… until he realized she was clutching a knife.

"Back away," she ordered. "Are you a thief?"

"I'm Ollie."

"Alright, Ollie," she said. "That still doesn't explain why you're poking around my camp in the middle of the night."

"I'm an astronomer," he said, lifting up his telescope case.

"Likely story."

"I swear."

"Prove it," she said.

Olivier laid his case on the salt and snapped open the latches. With the speed of a soldier assembling a rifle, he constructed his Criterion Dynascope and pointed it into the starry dynamo. He asked her what she wanted to see.

"How about the Crab Nebula?" she said. "Seems fitting the way you skitter."

He toured the southeast quadrant of the night sky and found it in less than ten seconds. She told him to step away. She looked in the telescope.

"So, you're not a liar," she said, adjusting the focus ring. "That's good. I hate liars."

"What's your name?" Olivier asked.

"Vera," she said and sheathed her knife.

Olivier told her that he'd been helping oversee the construction of a deep-space telescope array at the Cerro Tololo Observatory. She told him she'd been volunteering for the ESO at the La Silla Observatory while on sabbatical from the University of Amsterdam where she taught astrophysics. She eventually warmed to his presence after watching him shiver out on the salt for thirty minutes of her interrogation. She lent him a blanket and invited him to join her.

She showed him a small cylindrical device wired to a portable black-box computer console. She mounted the device onto an optical outlet underneath the eyepiece of her telescope.

"What does it do?" Olivier asked.

"It's a little complicated to explain. Let's just say it collects starlight so I can analyze it."

Olivier laughed. "That tiny gadget?"

"Wait for it."

An indicator light on the console began to glow, the monitor reporting data on the wavelength, spectra, and frequencies of the starlight. She showed him the different values she could analyze.

"It's a fancy spectrometer?"

"A spectrophotometer, a miniature version of the massive spectrograph we're working on at La Silla in collaboration with CERN. It uses fiber optics. I designed it myself."

"Can I ask you favor?" he said.

"Depends."

"Show me Beta Lyrae."

She angled the telescope and isolated the star in the constellation of Lyra. She punched away at the console. She looked at the read-out—an intense spectra with erratic fluctuations in wavelength and frequency.

"Hmm, that's a peculiar star," she said.

"I know," he said. "It's a dancer."

They shared a can of black beans and their favorite stars in the Southern Hemisphere above them. They talked about new galaxies, star systems, exoplanets discovered by telescopes around the world, trading facts and figures on the discoveries and the marvelous technology that made it possible. She told him she envied his life of travel. She often felt like an imposter in the rarified world of academia, having grown up on a farm in the Netherlands. And so, she escaped on adventures at every opportunity offered by the university.

Conversation was easy with her. They settled into a familiar cadence. It surprised him. Maybe it surprised her too. Eventually she told him he was welcome to camp with her if he agreed to maintain a gentlemanly distance, not so subtly reminding him that she had a knife and wasn't afraid to use it.

The next morning, they walked the salt flats together. She asked him if he'd been south to Patagonia. He told her no.

"Wanna go?" she asked. "I wouldn't mind the company if you wanted to tag along."

For most of Olivier's life, his neuroses had guided his decision-making. Running through probabilities, seeking counsel in the stars, listening to the tolling bell in his mind, saying now, now, now, behold the arrow of time, the splitting paths before you, choose the right one. He had no thoughts, gazing into Vera's imploring eyes. Instantly, he said yes.

They drove out through the desert to Santiago, then down Chile's green spine to Parque National Corcovado, the vivid colors of its wilderness iced with the enchanted breath of milky blue rivers and lakes. Three weeks of grease and sweat in the mythic land of giants, their clothes soiled, muscles exhausted from the changing temperatures. They hopped on a scientific boat at Puerto Cisnes, heading south through the green wonderland of glacial isles. Each time, after a few days at a destination, Vera would turn with a daring smirk and suggest they go farther.

A curious and vexing thing happened during their treks through the wild wild south of Patagonia. What he first perceived as frankly annoying idiosyncrasies—how she sang in the morning while boiling water for their instant coffee, how she spoke to the birds and wild animals on the rocky trails as if she knew their names, how she would sprint off like a child, excited by yet another masterpiece lookout in the living painting through which they hiked and he would worry, seriously worry, about her getting hurt—they all became endearing. There were days he'd wake up in awe of her as much as the enthralling mountains and grasslands at the end of the world. She was a mischievous contradiction—this serious physicist with heartful reverence for the mystery of the unknown. She loved mythology and astrology, often going off on divergent lectures on the ancient stories written in the constellations and why planetary alignments and moon phases mattered.

Olivier had his own fuzzy ideas on the enigmatic clockwork of the universe in addition to manifestation, multiverses, and the fundamental nature of consciousness from his psychedelic epiphanies and travels throughout Asia. One night, after skinny dipping in a cold lake at Torre del Plaine, they were laying out on the rocks under the stars when Vera noticed the ying-yang necklace on Olivier's hairy chest.

"What is that hippie thing anyway?" she teased him.

"It's a Taoist medallion," he said, somewhat

embarrassed. He went on to explain that he'd become fascinated with the hermit poet Lao Tzu and his natural theology during his time in China, spending many afternoons of tranquil respite at the White Cloud Temple in Shanghai. "The Eastern perspective is much more in line, you know, with your wacky world of subatomic physics."

"So you're a Taoist?"

"I'm wary of 'isms'. I don't subscribe to any ideology. I'm a knowledge seeker. More things in heaven and earth than dreamed in any philosophy."

"He quotes the bard. How adorable." Vera smiled. "Are you religious, Ollie?"

"Not if I can help it," Olivier said. "I used to think the universe was kind. Now I think it's just indifferent."

"That's why I have to get out of the lab. I spend so much time observing these misbehaving particles that I often feel removed from it. Equations, abstractions. The shape of things we cannot see. Out here... I'm swept away. Growing up Catholic, I always thought religion was so dogmatic and boring. But when I started studying astronomy, it awakened something within me. So, I invented my own religion."

"Oh really?" Olivier said. "And what's that?"

"It's kind of embarrassing, but I'm a romantic," she said. "I imagine the universe as a goddess with three attendant deities: Love, Beauty, and Truth. The beauty of cosmos... its immaculate symmetries, asymmetries, mathematical equations distilled to perfect expressions. The paradoxical truth that one equals infinity, multitudes within multitudes, who we are, what we are, trying to make sense of the mystery above and below..."

"You skipped love," Olivier said.

"That's what binds us, connects us, makes us human. Grounds our feet to the earth."

"Are you positing that love is gravity?"

She laughed. "Who knows? Maybe that's the elusive relation between gravity and the electromagnetic field. The weight of love and its kinetics. Maybe planets fall in love with a star and that's why we're all spinning."

There was a six-month flurry of letters and phone calls after their Patagonia trip until they decided to meet again and travel to Iceland. Thus began a decade of adventure together. Tanzania, Vietnam, Ecuador, Nepal, Hawaii. Although he was loath to admit it then, fiercely protective of his independence and fearful of the nascent song in his heart, it was without a doubt the happiest time of his life.

5.

IN the summer of 1994, Olivier was laying low in a seaside bungalow on Monterey beach, hired by a former colleague from Mount Wilson to help set up a private array of telescopes for a stargazing retreat at the Esalen Institute in Big Sur.

The phone rang. He immediately recognized the melodic cadence of her voice.

"New Zealand?" he asked again.

"Yes," she said. "Sounds fun, right? Want to come?"

He made excuses to leave his job a week early and hopped three planes over the vast forever blue Pacific and its jigsaw islands to meet Vera in Auckland. It had been almost two years since he'd last seen her. With his ankles swollen stepping down off the plane and his heart swollen with the anticipation of seeing her again, Olivier told himself he wouldn't run away this time. He would face his fear and tell her. Maybe they would settle down in Belgium or the Netherlands and raise a family together. They weren't too old yet. He ignored the daily horoscopes and their cryptic nonsense about the thorns of a stubborn rose.

He found himself, emboldened and jet-lagged, riding in a campervan across the ever-green fjords of New Zealand's South Island. Vera, with her blonde hair wild in the wind, kept her white-gloved hands gripped on the wheel, masterfully dodging sheep on the road, en route to the observatory on Mount John. They were treated to a tour of the facilities by Dr. Laura Gottfried, a former colleague of Vera's from the University of Amsterdam, even though its interstellar microlensing telescope was under maintenance. Over a lunch of meat pies and honey-drizzled kiwi, Dr. Gottfried recommended a campsite in the foothills of Mitre Peak where the mountains cradled the valley and created a natural amphitheater. The best place to witness the New Zealand night sky, Dr. Gottfried said.

And so, Vera and Olivier drove the corkscrew roads through the narrow mountain passes, rising in elevation as sundown blessed the fjords and lush green hills with a violet luster, the van's motor working overtime. They detoured through the high grass onto a ridge with a clear view of Mitre Peak over the Milford Sound. Twilight eclipsed the valley and cast the hills in darkness. They waited in breathless awe for the stars.

They set up camp on the ridge, pitching stakes in the pure dark, nothing but shadowed peaks and starlight. They cooked sausages that night too, huddled around a fire.

"There was a falcon, remember?" Olivier recalled, fifteen years later, turning over the blistered sausages on the hot-plate stove in his room at the Port d'Etoile. Vera sat on his unmade bed, petting Tiku.

"Was there?" she asked.

"Yes, you were waxing philosophique on a myth—"

"Me? Never."

"…about how one of the constellations came to be named… Oh yes, Perseid. I was pretending like I hadn't heard your theory before."

"That's one of my better ones. The Perseid meteoroids as drops of blood from Medusa's severed head, falling from the heavens and birthing Pegasus."

"You can always count on the Greeks to take something beautiful and make it bloody," Olivier said. "You really don't remember the falcon? This terrifying winged shadow soared out over us while we were eating supper, so large it obscured the stars."

"Ha, I totally forgot," she said. "That scared the hell out of me."

"Yeah, you dropped your sausage, and it rolled downhill off the ridge!"

Olivier didn't tell her the rest of it. How he clasped her shoulder on instinct. How his grip softened, his arms relaxed, a nervous ecstasy feeling her warmth. How they settled into each other, laughing away their fright, once again alone with the looming peaks in the lustrous dew of night. How their eyes met in the dark, his heart pounding in its prison, yearning to break free with the confession of a kiss. And then he froze, paralyzed by a fear of the unknown. They'd been friends for so long. He didn't want to complicate things. Their affection felt so natural in its innocence. It was a risk with too many variables to calculate, known and unknown. After all, what did she really think of him? He could never read her. Was he even worthy of her? And now, decades later, he felt overcome by the same pain and nostalgia, a longing to find a home in her heart. The same urgency, the same impulse to release the birdsong of his soul, the mockingbird chitter that keep him awake, singing off-key in the long wan night.

Olivier turned off the burner. He didn't want to spoil the mood. She was radiant with a savage joy, biting into the juicy sausages. She licked the drippings from her fingertips. He was so captivated by her hunger that he didn't even worry about the grease splatter on his bedspread.

"Thank you for the letter, Ollie," she said. "I'm sorry I haven't stayed in touch."

Olivier sat down beside her with another plate of sausages. "Where'd you have the wedding?"

"Oh, it was a small ceremony at a castle outside Wiesbaden. Mostly family."

"A castle?" Olivier scoffed. "Of course, anything less would be gauche and unbefitting of a Konigsmann wedding."

"Don't be mean," she said. "I wanted to invite you. I was just worried about what might happen, considering you tried to strangle Fritz the last time he was here."

"We were wrestling. We were drunk. It was nothing."

"You were jealous. It's natural."

"Jealous? I wasn't jealous."

"Let's not get into it." She flicked her hand, shards of light sparkling off her diamond ring. "I want to hear about you. Tell me about your adventures in the desert."

Olivier ate his sausages and unwound story after

story of his road trips throughout the Draa Valley—Aït Mansour, Tamegroute, Kasbah de Caids. Tall tales of cultural mishaps, unexpected discoveries, accidental heroics. She knew half his stories were fantasy, the truth stretched to its hyperbolic limit. She didn't seem to care.

"Of course, that was before my car rusted out. Nothing survives the grit out here," Olivier said. "Aside from trips into town with the hotel porters, I've been stuck with only my telescopes and little Tiku for company."

"Ah, but she's so cute." Vera scooped the kitten into her lap. "Why would you ever want to leave?" The tabby cat sprawled out between her legs and purred.

"I heard you left CERN," Olivier said.

"I did," she said, stroking Tiku's fur. "It wasn't an easy decision. I really loved it there, but I felt like much of my work was done once we successfully activated the Hadron Collider. The rest is just research, which doesn't excite me as much as designing instruments for observation. Now I'm one of the lead astrophysics engineers at ESTEC in Noordwijk, believe it or not."

"You're living in the Netherlands?" he said, rolling a cigarette.

"Well, I was spending the week there and weekends in Potsdam. But I don't feel comfortable being away from Fritz for long anymore. I'm mostly working remote and only traveling to the institute when they really need me." Vera scratched behind the kitten's ears. "How's your research on Beta Lyrae and your misbehaving binaries?"

He spun the tobacco and licked the paper. "I gave up on that long ago."

"Oh Ollie, that's sad," she said. "It's a beautiful theory. I think about it all the time. I want to believe it's true."

"So do I." Olivier lit his cigarette and blew smoke out the window. Vera asked if she could have a drag.

"I thought you quit," he said.

"I'm full of surprises," she said with a wink. He passed over the thin cigarette, their fingers brushing. She pulled delicately and exhaled a lazy whirl into the dusty air.

"Is that?" She pointed across the bedroom at the mason jar on the bookshelf. "Is it—?"

"Dead? Good question." Olivier received the cigarette back from her. He smoked, eying the black scorpion. There were many times he'd assumed it dead, posed for days on end with hardly any movement. But whenever he stared long and hard at the scorpion, it woke and twitched, striking its tail at the glass. An invitation, a dare. The easy way out. One strike from its thorn was all it would take, the venom seeping into his blood, restricting his ventricles and throttling his weary heart. Androctonus maurtanicus. Death in a glass cage.

"I doubt it," he said. "Those buggers would survive a nuclear apocalypse."

Vera rose from the bed and approached the bookshelf, fascinated by the ancient predator in the glass jar. Olivier told her the story of his heroic capture of the mythic assassin, how he very nearly avoided being stung, and so on, with a few minor embellishments.

What he didn't tell her was how he showed the scorpion to the hotel porters—a bunch of local boys who also helped with cleaning and kitchen duties under the supervision of Madame Habib. They were delighted by his treasure, especially Amadou with whom Olivier had a friendly relationship despite the fact he was Moussa's nephew. It was from Amadou that he learned scorpion venom was one of the most valuable liquids in the world because of its use by the pharmaceutical industry, fetching thousands of dollars for tiny vials of it. And so, with the promise of money at hand, Amadou convinced Olivier to let him milk the scorpion with a nine-volt battery and pair of hookah tongs.

"It's dreadful and gorgeous," Vera said.

"One of the many excitements of the desert. There are a hundred ways to die out here," Olivier said. "The yellow ones are more common. Black scorpions are mostly found farther out in the Sahara."

Vera resettled on the bed. Olivier could sense her unease… or was it genuine fear? How strange this seemed coming from her. Vera, the adventurer. Vera, the dauntless. Vera, the trailblazer who always raced toward the edge of danger with a mischievous joy, eager to bushwhack into the unknown on their treks together for the thrill of discovering some remote lookout in the wilderness, a vantage point of the cosmos rarely seen before.

She slipped the cigarette from his fingers. Their eyes met quite suddenly. She shied away. She took a leisurely drag with a pensive quixotic intensity.

"Have you ever been to the Chegaga Dunes?" she asked.

"Once," Olivier said. It hadn't been a pleasant experience out in the endless sand of those gigantic otherworldly dunes on the border of Algeria. He didn't like to think about it.

She passed the cigarette. "Fritz wants to go."

"I'm sure Moussa could arrange a trip for him," Olivier said. "Have fun with the nomads. They hate foreigners or anyone who bathes regularly."

"He wants you to come."

"Why?" Olivier asked.

"He wants to see the stars out there. The Voyager is too big and delicate to be transported in a jeep for hours into the dunes. He's hoping you might be willing to come."

"It doesn't matter what I want." Olivier stubbed his cigarette out in an empty beer can. "I know my role."

"Oh, come on, Ollie." Vera gently touched his arm. "It'll be fun, I swear. An adventure, like old times."

6.

OLIVIER had sworn he would never return to the Chegaga Dunes after the disaster of his first and only excursion out into the Sahara. Shortly after he'd started his tenure as resident astronomer at the Port d'Etoile, he had traveled with Karl on a bonding adventure to see the famous dunes. On their way into the desert, they had stopped at one of the oases separated by miles and miles of sand. They were greeted by nomads on camelback. Olivier had read that it was bad luck not to give the nomads a small token of appreciation if you crossed paths in the desert. A tribute for safe passage. He had watched as Karl shook the nomad's hand and slipped him a dirham in thanks.

After an uneventful night of camping, the stars spoiled by clouds, they stopped for tea with an elderly nomadic goat herder and his wife on their way home from the dunes. Olivier saw this as his moment to ingratiate himself with the lords of the desert. He reached out to shake the old man's boney hand with a dirham cupped in his palm. The instant the old man felt the copper, he whipped his hand away as if he'd been hexed. His rheumy eyes recoiled in horror, his mouth clenched. The coin twirled in the air and plopped in the sand.

Olivier spent the rest of their visit, cross-legged in the sand, drinking tea and scraping off goat scat from his sandals, as Karl soothed the old man's anger, trying to convince him that Olivier hadn't just tried to bribe him into selling off his herd.

Somehow against all protests—objections denied, excuses invalidated—Olivier was enlisted to accompany the astronomers on their five-hour journey to the end of the Draa Valley and out into the dunes of the Sahara beyond. Only half the entourage had decided to go—Ingrid, Allister, Saul, Fritz, and Vera piling into two flattop 4x4 jeeps.

The road was hazy in the coughing dawn, the rosy light of a new day gritted by a rolling storm of gravel and sand kicked up by their caravan. Olivier, hungover and looking like a washed-up rockstar in his boonie hat and yellow aviators, was crammed with Saul in the back of the jeep at the rear of the caravan. Behind the wheel, Amadou, who'd contracted a local desert safari company for their overnight excursion and no doubt pocketed the commission, deflected chitchat from Ingrid in the passenger seat since he didn't speak German. He politely nodded at her questions and gestured off at the barren scenery of rock and sand and desolate highway to distract her.

Half an hour later, the desert caravan made a brief stop on the palm-tree main road in Zagora to stock up on supplies. All eyes of the town were on the European fish out of water. Dour mustached men smoking cigarettes outside the cafes. Darting eyes of women in hijabs sweeping dust out of stores. Curious barefoot children flitting in and out of sandstone archways.

It was the offseason after a bad year for tourism. Towns like Zagora survived on the tour buses from Marrakesh and the gullible cash-flush tourists who paid them a small fortune in dirhams for babouches, cheap dyed scarfs, fake Berber jewelry, fire-scorched watercolor paintings. The high-profile murder of a Spanish university student had made the Europeans less inclined to holiday in Morocco. Olivier could sense their sharklike desperation. Narrow eyes that would grow wide with a broad smile whenever you said hello. The wider the smile, the sharper the knife, or so the old saying went in the desert.

Olivier always considered the Draa Valley more dangerous than the rest of Morocco. It was true that in the stonewalled medinas of Marrakesh and Fez there was a grinning madness of counterfeit hawkers, swindlers in the souks, leatherman con-artists, obnoxious gangs of teenagers in the labyrinthine streets. Elsewhere in the seaside towns on the coast, the mountain villages of the midlands, the verdant hills and valleys of the north, the locals were some of the most generous, kind, and thoughtful people he'd ever met. A culture of hospitality, sharing what little they had with neighbors and strangers alike.

But something happened in the heat of the Draa Valley. A parch-mouthed hunger in the no man's land of the Sahara. The ethical code of society abandoned for a more succinct set of rules: survive through cunning or perish with no one to bury your bones but the sand.

The store clerk loaded up a cardboard box of apricots, figs, biscuit crackers, and bottled water. Moussa haggled over the price. The store clerk threw his hands in the air and cursed under his breath. Fritz brought everyone headscarves and postcards with a fistful of cash.

"Shukran." The clerk grinned. "Where are you headed?"

"The Chegaga Dunes," Fritz said.

"Ah, yes…" the clerk then spoke aside to Moussa in Arabic. Something about nomads, petty grievances, questions about who their host was in the desert. Moussa mentioned a name. The clerk shook his head and offered a different name. He slipped out a business card from under the cash register. Moussa argued but pocketed the card anyway. The clerk held up his finger and went into the storage room. He returned with a flayed goat head wrapped in plastic.

He smiled wide. "A gift for supper. Tell Youssef I say hello."

✻

THE highway breeze whipped through the canopy of the jeep, Saul coughing into his scarf from diesel fumes and dust, Olivier queasy from the stench of the goat head between his legs. He was careful not to let his ankles touch the slimy plastic. He pretended this didn't bother him. He goaded Amadou into turning on the radio to Chada FM, which sometimes played the electrified Taureg and Algerian rock and blues that was popular with teenagers farther south where the post-colonial rebellions of the 1960s had never really ended. A distorted twang of dueling guitars drifted from the radio. The dreams, hopes, and angst of the youth amplified and carried on a short-wave frequency— three decades of fighting for independence, followed by another decade of civil war, and all the people ever wanted was peace and a simple life.

Olivier unzipped the front pocket on his denim jacket. He slipped out a joint and sparked it.

"Want some hashish?" he whispered, offering Saul the joint.

"Yes, please. Just don't tell the others." He winked and puffed away. "What is this music? It's amazing."

"Sahel rock. Music of revolution," Olivier said.

"Man, this is so good," Saul said.

"It's the best," Olivier said. "Six-string sorcerers. They play like they're casting spells."

In the jeep ahead of them, Moussa was driving like a goat herder, swerving around potholes, the silver-streaked kite of Vera's hair dancing in the breeze, Fritz gleeful in movie-star sunglasses with his arm wrapped around her. Olivier could feel the distance between himself and her physical presence broaden and deepen like a chasm. In its place, a desperate longing, like the desert itself, as full as it was empty. An intense attraction, a magnetism to her electrical field, that had rendered him frenzied from sitting in such close proximity the night before. Or perhaps it was something more mystical, he let himself imagine. Her prana, her ruah, her orenda, her qi, or any of the other names that cultures from time immemorial gave to the cosmic wind and breath of life, the unnamable energy that flows through all things and their eternal interconnectedness.

With this yearning came an unruly wrath and its possession. Fritz had known how much he cared for Vera. Olivier must have confessed his feelings a thousand times to his old friend over pints in the brauhaus whenever he visited him in Potsdam. Fritz had always responded with his sonorous laugh, pushing Olivier with haughty platitudes to admit that he may need someone in his life. Then there was that night in Geneva five years ago when he'd returned from Morocco for a short stay in Europe. Vera had been hired as an Applied Physicist at CERN. Fritz had been in the city for an astronomy conference. After a tour of the Large Hadron Collider, the three of them had gone out to dinner together. Olivier thought nothing at first of the way they'd decided to sit next to each other at the table. He knew they'd become close acquaintances. Vera had worked briefly at the Leibniz Institute of Astrophysics. Fritz had been instrumental in helping her secure a position on the Hadron Collider project. Late that night, Olivier had insinuated to his old friend that he still had feelings for her. Fritz's response was blunt and strange—well, you better do something about it, or somebody else will.

Olivier hadn't considered this a threat at the time. Then came those months of silence… from her, from him. Maybe he had made things worse on Fritz's last visit to the Port d'Etoile. Maybe he could've had a more mature reaction when Fritz told him that he and Vera were dating instead of tossing wine in his face and challenging him to a wrestling match, as he had many times during their school days at the Sorbonne when one of Fritz's pranks went too far. Maturity, arguably, was neither of their strong suits.

What was most infuriating though was Fritz's expectation of forgiveness without any expression of remorse. Olivier had only demanded an earnest apology, an explanation. Then the shock of it, learning of their imminent betrothal on scented cardstock in a formal exaltation of the happy couple's undying love. An engagement? After only a year? He'd held out hope that she'd call it off, that she'd grow tired of Fritz's goofy charms, his childishness, his self-absorbed entitlement.

Now, upon the return of the esteemed Dr. Konigsmann, a sinister desire possessed Olivier of equal weight to his longing—the fantasy of revenge made manifest in the 1.25 milligrams of black scorpion venom capped in a vial and stowed away with his telescope. He'd done the calculations. It wasn't enough to kill Fritz, but it sure as hell was enough to make him suffer.

The jeep lurched into a higher gear on the open road. The goat head flopped on its side. Olivier placed it upright again between his ankles and felt something furry graze his leg. Flash of a tail. He craned forward to find Tiku curled under his seat.

"A stowaway." Saul grinned. "Is she yours? She's darling."

Olivier put a finger to his lips, then pointed at the red fez bobbing in the jeep ahead of them. If Moussa found out the cat had hitched a ride, he'd surely conspire some way to get rid of Tiku for good, even if that meant throwing her in a ditch on the desert highway.

Civilization crumbled to dust along the lone road south of Tamegroute, a regression thousands of years back in time. The sandstone of desert villages scuttled to rubble, the pastel colors blanched to an all-too familiar shade of beige. Quivering chimera in the heat. There was no one on the road except for sandal-footed travelers emerging from the dust on the side of the highway. Artisans in hooded cloaks with donkeys saddled with clay jugs, lanterns, rugs. The Berber way of life. Sometimes Olivier felt envious of their freedom. How simply they lived, carrying on centuries-old traditions of craftsmanship, living on nothing more than the handful of dirhams they made walking for miles between villages to barter and trade.

The sun had reached its broiling point at high noon when the caravan coasted through the last vestige of civilization, a ghost town scattered with goats and a few villagers resting under the shade of wilted palm trees.

"What town is this?" Ingrid asked from the front seat.

"M'Hamid," Amadou replied. "End of road."

"They seem afraid of us," Saul said.

"They are wary," Olivier said. "They have a healthy mistrust of foreigners."

He went on to explain that the Saharan border between Morocco and Algeria had been in dispute since the Algerian revolution. After decades of bloodshed, the locals were just trying to live their quiet lives in the desert, unbothered.

"That's terrible," Saul said.

"What's worse is that the French and Spanish may have left years ago, but the European imperialists are still colonializing through their influence," Olivier told him. "After losing their ancestral land, these people are now worried about losing their culture. Their kids don't care about crafting, trading, or learning the Berber ways. They listen to rock 'n' roll, watch YouTube, complain about spotty Wi-Fi like the foreigners. These people have every reason to hate us."

They passed a final signpost in Arabic, an exclamation point within a red triangle. The road disintegrated into isthmus patches of tar, the jeeps rocking in the wake, the shocks unforgiving, the wheels finally finding traction on the coarse red sand scattered with black pebbles.

"Good? Ready?" Amadou barked over his shoulder in broken English.

He gripped the wheel and barreled out across the boundless expanse of sand, charging at full speed through the smoking heat of the desert.

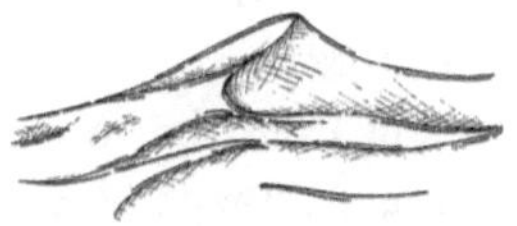

7.

THE Sahara swept its ancient sand in a blind compass, the horizon a vague sun-scorched whiteout of shimmering light. Nothing but sand for miles and miles, a broken hourglass of time, all history buried in the rock dust, the millennium of life on earth laid waste as if it never happened. It was the closest any of the astronomers would come to an extraterrestrial landscape. Olivier thought of Mars, Venus, Jupiter and the millions of other inhospitable planets out there in the anonymity of space. The desert morphed before their eyes like a surreal dream—the hard scrabble of molten rocks and fossils, craters of scrub brush, humps of dunes that the jeeps rumbled up and over, lurching off sideways, wheels spinning in the air and sinking into soft earth, making waves in the ocean of sand.

They drove for two hours straight, stopping only once to wash the grit from their faces at an oasis in the vast interminable desert. Amadou hauled up buckets of water from a stone well as the astronomers waited patiently in the hot sun, eyes stinging, sweat congealed on their foreheads.

Their presence did not go unnoticed by the lords of the desert. Moussa waved his fez cap and walked out to meet the curious nomads who rode out on camelback from a tuft of palm trees in the distance. The nomads slowed their trot and eyed the foreigners from afar. They shouted at Moussa. They did not dismount. No handshakes. No glint of coin or telltale smile. Amadou hooked the pulley rope and handed off the water bucket to Fritz. He rushed out with his arms raised in greeting, praising whatever God didn't melt under the unforgiving sun. There was a tense exchange with the nomads. Olivier didn't like the sound of it.

Back in the jeeps, the rolling caps of the Chegaga Dunes rose in the white heat. The desert softened with golden sand, the gargantuan dunes emerging from the fever dream into reality. The jeeps carved across the enormous waves of sand, churning their wheels up the wide crest and skating downhill to a basecamp in the valley of the first ridge. They parked outside some cinderblocks that marked the entrance. A shredded red flag sprouted from a pile of scrapyard junk like a wasteland flower.

"What is this place?" Saul asked, squinting under the fierce sun.

"Syrtis Major," Olivier joked and climbed out of the jeep. His sandals sunk deep into the warm sand. The dunes were objectively beautiful and unsettling. This monstrous granular sea. The immensity of it, the serenity of it. A sameness that made you feel lost standing still. It was somewhere you waited to be rescued, somewhere you waited to die.

He remembered the astonishing snapshots of Mars that the first rover Sojourner transmitted to Earth in 1996. He'd been one of the first to see them—vague flickering images on the NASA relay feed during his brief stint as a systems coordinator at the White Sands Observatory in New Mexico. A barren planet of nothing but boulders and red sand in an oppressive orange haze. The Sahara evoked the same terrifying feeling of total desolation.

Olivier leaned against the jeep. What was this place? It was a fair question. The basecamp was nothing more than a pair of rundown tents huddled around the char of a firepit. Off to the left, a tattered banquet tent with wooden chairs and a broad table on a camel-hair rug. Off to the right, a small patchwork tent with a stovepipe crooked out the roof. Someone was snoring inside. The astronomers waited while Amadou went in to rouse their host.

Vera helped Fritz wrap a purple scarf around his head in a traditional Berber style. He wriggled as she fussed with the fabric, the revered astronomer reduced to a giddy teenager in his whirlwind of excitement. As soon as she was done, Fritz scampered away and hiked up the steep dune with Ingrid, Saul, and Allister.

Olivier lowered the back gate of the jeep. With caution, he pulled out a black case that contained his Criterion Dynascope. Tiku poked out from under the seat. Her soft yellow eyes inquired whether it was safe to come out. Olivier shook a finger. She slinked under the seat again. He lifted off the case and closed the gate.

"This is incredible. It's like something out of Lawrence of Arabia," Fritz yelled down from the ridge. "What do you think, Ollie?" He flashed a wide grin, his broad Roman nose in profile with the pure blue sky and sea of dunes.

"A modern-day Peter O'Toole," Olivier shouted back. He secreted the case away behind the jeep and unlatched it in the sand. The telescope was intact, protected in padded foam, no damage from its rocky voyage across the Sahara. He then glanced around to make sure nobody was watching. He peeled the foam from the right corner. There were no visible cracks in the milky vial underneath, nor the fat mason jar wedged beside it, although its prisoner was visibly agitated. The black scorpion pinged at the glass with its stinger.

"Careful there. Watch yourself."

Olivier startled and turned. Vera was floating in the desert heat on the dune slope, tying off her red headscarf. "Your Flanders skin is frying up."

He pretended to inspect the telescope and discreetly smoothed out the foam. If she'd seen anything, her face did not betray it. He latched the case shut.

"Sorry, what's that?"

"Your neck. It's scarlet. It's painful just looking at you," she said. "Come here."

She fetched a headscarf from the jeep and beckoned him closer. He rose from the sand, blinded by the bright sun. She took off his boonie hat. Her hands brushed his shoulders, looping the thin scarf around his bushy grey hair, under his collar, tucking loose fabric behind his ears. Every time her fingertips touched his skin it sent a prickling warmth through his body like electricity through a live wire.

"There you are," she said, placing the hat back on his head. "Ready for adventure."

There was a clanging of pots and muffled voices inside the small tent. Amadou emerged from the flap with a bowl of fruit, followed by an old man in a hooded cloak.

Fritz and the rest of the astronomers scrambled down from the dune. Amadou whispered in Moussa's ear.

"This is Youssef," Moussa said. "Our gracious host."

The astronomers shook hands with the old man and introduced themselves.

"A rider is en route with the camels. In the meantime, Youssef has brewed some tea and would like us to make ourselves at home."

Youssef nodded as if he understood every word spoken in the foreign tongue. There were sandbags under his eyes, his broad smile freighted by a general weariness. Amadou brought the goat head from the jeep. Youssef accepted the slimy plastic bag, drops of watery blood leaking on the sand. He gestured for his guests to go inside.

*

THE astronomers enjoyed afternoon tea in the banquet tent while they waited for the camels that would carry them farther into the desert. Most of the group sat cross-legged on the rug since there were only three chairs around the table. Youssef poured mint tea from a stone teapot, effortlessly moving the arc of steaming hot water between the clay cups, raising and lowering the spout to cool off the tea. His guests were delighted by the parlor trick. Moussa ate a handful of almonds and checked his pocket watch. Olivier eyed Youssef with trepidation, worried his shaky grip might slip and splash scalding hot water in their laps. Fritz sipped his tea and instantly proclaimed it was the best he'd ever tasted.

Something was strange about their host, how he refused to connect with anyone's eyes. The curious scars on his knuckles, the ragged camelhair of his Berber cloak like a costume dusted off from the closet of a shuttered community theater, leaving a cloud of dander in his wake. Yet the astronomers were unaffected by his bizarre appearance, the stifling flat heat in the tent, the musty smell of rot and mold. They were gliding on the bullish winds of their adventure, enchanted by the Sahara, lost in the magic of the strange dunes.

It was just shy of sundown when the camels arrived, the fiery red sun setting the dunes ablaze as the astronomers saddled onto the humps and departed from the base camp. The master of the camels was a handsome young nomad in a matching blue headscarf and robe who led the expedition. The camels were obedient and trotted single file at a slow pace over the gigantic dunes.

Olivier rode the runt of the litter, a scrawny camel with a bad haircut. The poor animal wheezed under the weight of his precious cargo—the black case roped to the saddle and the rebellious kitten smuggled in his rucksack. He trailed in the rear so Tiku could poke her head out and enjoy glimpses of their trek across the vast expanse of nothing.

The desert was a wondrous place to visit and a

terrifying place to know. The sun burning through the blanched sky, the rise and fall of the tremendous dunes, the never-ending sand and its crowned horizons. It was a miracle anything survived in the Sahara. But sure enough, there were wildflower sprigs in the valleys of the dunes, blue-shelled beetles that made racing tracks in the sand. He even saw a lizard dart under his camel's legs.

Olivier would have never suspected that there could be life this far out. But life in and of itself was improbable, wasn't it? 4 billion years ago when carbon-hydrogen molecules first evolved into microbial cells, squirmy cytoplasm with membranes, gaining complexity. The same magic trick that the cosmic jester pulled during the Big Bang, a quantum acceleration of thermodynamic complexity that gave birth to billions of galaxies and the wonder of planets, infinitely diverse, orbiting suns of their own across the dark universe. Molten rock, sulfuric clouds, oceans of ice, endless deserts.

The sun torched the horizon in a slow burn. The nomad in the blue kaftan played a few pretty notes on a reed flute and the camels halted their single-file march. The astronomers clapped in delight and dismounted. They climbed for a view of the sunset on a colossal dune, in the immense desert, on this lonely planet spinning, the mother star seemingly melting beyond the horizon line, the sky and sand radiated with an intense nuclear red glow. Fritz clomped along the ridgeline in his boots, shooting the panorama with a hulking DSLR camera. Vera sat by herself in contemplation.

"Do you mind if I sit?" Olivier asked.

She hushed him, patting the sand beside her.

Olivier sat down, conscious of her energy, conscious of his every movement, slowing his heavy breaths from the climb. She used to get furious with him for clumsiness, usually after one of his many haphazard accidents during their adventures. How he almost tripped down the stone stairs in Goa, how he spilled his cocktail on the illustrious Dr. Covington during a party in London, how he accidentally knocked over a fruit cart in St. Lucia. She used to say "pay attention… your head's always in the clouds… you're missing it" whenever he'd drift off into the deep space of his thoughts, often on their long drives together across the countryside of Mexico, Tanzania, Vietnam. "The universe is out there, not in here," she used to say, pointing at her head.

Olivier tried to concentrate on the sunset, but he was distracted by the intensity of her meditation, her eyes focused on the fiery horizon as if the world were ending, as if she were breaking down the atmospheric light into spectral wavelengths and absorbing the velocity. Alive, aware, and fully present in the moment.

Fritz returned and made himself a seat, kicking up a puff of sand.

"I think I got the perfect shot," he said.

"Shhh," she said, and the men sat perfectly still and perfectly silent beside her until long after the sun had disappeared behind the dunes.

8.

THEY journeyed on camelback into the twilight, the torched desert light of the swallowed sun evaporating into a cool vacuous night. Billions of stars emerged from the darkened strata like a shimmering mirage, infinity multiplied in time and space, deepening into a vast and messy unknown. They rode the shadow dunes into the dreamlike vista, upended into the stellar dome, craning their necks to take it all in while the camels plodded along dazed by the view. Whenever they slowed to a crawl, the nomad in the blue kaftan would blow on his reed flute in harsh staccato to shake the camels awake and resume their trek.

Lost somewhere between the desert and the stars, Olivier floated on the hump of his scrawny camel, trying to maintain his equilibrium. It was stunning, beyond anything he'd ever seen, ten times more brilliant than his outpost at the Port d'Etoile. The sky so transparent that you could see the true chaos of universe, the constellations blotched with clusters, tangled in milky bands of stardust, nebulae, remnants, all the interstellar fire and fury. He felt a rush and thrill witnessing the night sky painted in such mythic strokes. A flush of excitement quaked his nerves, despite himself, despite his cynicism, his burnt skin chilled in the quickly cooling night.

His camel grumbled and threatened to buck as Olivier wrestled off his rucksack and placed it in his lap. Tiku poked her furry head out to watch the show with him, like they did together almost every night on the hotel's roof. There was the Dog Star in Canis Major, Betelgeuse in the armor of Orion, M35 at Gemini's feet. The only comparable experience was Uluru in Australia or perhaps Namibia? He'd been so sick with dysentery during that trip that he dismissed half the blinking stars as fever-born delusions.

"There's IC 10," Fritz called out from the front of the pack, his boorish voice booming across the dunes. "It's clear as the Seven Sisters tonight."

"Cassiopeia is very sharp out here," Ingrid replied. "Fritz, did you bring the astrolabe you bought at Ait Benhaddou?"

"Indeed, I did. What better occasion to try it out!"

"It's junk," Allister said. "It's not real."

"You're just mad because I haggled the man down to 500 dirhams after you'd given up the fight."

"It's a reproduction."

"It's an heirloom! You heard the story. It was his great-grandfather's. He showed us the markings."

"You're so naïve. There's no way it's a hundred years old."

Fritz ignored the insult. "Oh, look at Vega. You can

see its rings!" He then turned and hollered behind him.
"Ollie, are you seeing this? You still back there? Is your
camel dead?"

"I'm here," Olivier shouted.

"Well, keep up, my good man. Don't go getting
yourself lost in the desert."

Vera, saddled behind her husband on their camel,
turned her attention from the stars. She glanced over
her shoulder, a momentary flicker of her light traveling
over the dunes, searching the shadows for him, across
the grey expanse of sand, shining star to shining star
lost in the darkness. She hugged her arms around Fritz's
waist as the camel descended a steep bank.

Olivier was in no rush to catch up. He lingered in
the rear with Saul, passing the nub of the joint between
camels, dumbstruck with utter delight at the starlit
voyage through the sea of dunes. Saul toked and exhaled
out into the lustrous night.

"You're in love with her," he said with a wry smile.

"We're just old friends," Olivier said.

"Sure." Saul winked. "You never know what the stars
might have mapped out for you."

*

THEY made camp in a flat belly between two giant
dunes, their peaks carving into the sky like the walls of
an ancient alien citadel. The nomad in the blue kaftan
set about with his reed flute commanding the camels
to buckle and kneel so the astronomers could safely
dismount. Olivier hitched on his rucksack and untied
the black case from the saddle. He patted his camel's

mohawk, which elicited a high-pitch wheeze and blubbering from the grumpy animal that he interpreted as an enduring sign of friendship.

Moussa oversaw the pitching of the tents, fast and steady work done by Amadou and the nomad, erecting their tiny camp under the stars. Olivier asked the nomad in Arabic if he needed any help with the tents. He looked up, confused, staking the desert and unfurling canvas. Olivier asked the question again. The nomad shook his head and gestured for Moussa.

"What you want, Ollie?" Moussa said.

"I was just asking if he wanted a hand securing the tent poles," Olivier said.

"Actually, you asked whether he wanted your hands to work his pole," Moussa said. "Let them do their job and you do yours. I imagine our guests might enjoy a little stargazing after supper, don't you think?"

"Oh shoot, I forgot to bring my telescope," Olivier said. "Should I go back and get it?"

Moussa glared, stone-faced at the shaggy stoned astronomer. "You're joking."

"You're learning," Olivier said. "You know someday you may develop a sense of humor and grow to like me."

"I doubt that," he said.

Olivier climbed up a dune on the far side of camp with his cargo. Reaching the summit, he looked down at the astronomers waiting in the valley of the twin dunes like patient tourists, staring into infinity. Olivier wished he could join them. He felt apart from the group, like a Martian alone in the craters of Syrtis Major, spying on visitors to his desert planet. No matter how much Fritz and his friends pretended Olivier was their equal, the truth remained, an itchy sensation of otherness. They were a constellation of brilliant minds, and he was a lonely dwarf star in some remote quadrant of the galaxy. What had he ever achieved beyond his own delusions of grandeur?

He set down the black case in the deep soft sand. Tiku rumbled about in his rucksack.

"Alright, you little furball," Olivier said, loosening the cinch. "Behave. We can't let Moussa see you."

The tabby cat wiggled out of the rucksack. She yawned, crinkling her nose, and stretched her legs. Olivier pulled out a tuna can and peeled off the tab. Tiku sniffed the tin. She tongued the top layer of gelatinous fat, losing interest after a few licks. She pawed the sand and tested her steps on the slope.

"Don't go too far, okay?" he said. "And stay away from the campfire."

Tiku flailed her tail, defiant and playful, and wandered off down the dune.

Olivier opened the black case and began to assemble the telescope. Kneeling in the sand, he secured the viewfinder onto his Criterion Dynascope. He sunk the tripod legs deep into the desert and made slight tweaks to the height. He zeroed in on M42, the Orion Nebula, which was impressively colorful and without its usual muddiness. He then left the telescope alone, stabilized and ready in case anyone came looking for him.

At his sandaled feet, the empty black case lay open, his secrets buried within. He dug his fingers into the seams and slipped out the vial from its hiding place. It was only a sampling of the venom he had milked from the scorpion with Amadou who'd yet to find a buyer for the rare toxin. He could hear its owner stir underneath the foam padding, clinking in the mason jar.

He hadn't intended to bring the scorpion, but now it seemed a fitting gesture to return the servant of death to its homeland. Like the plan itself, it was an accumulation of impulsive decisions that snowballed from the nagging idea of it. Some small foolish notion of revenge, sitting in his room with his frazzled nerves, after seeing her, after seeing him, after seeing them together again. An old wound enflamed, the stitches undone. And then he'd heard the scorpion skitter in its jar on the bookshelf like it was scratching an itch. The bell began to toll in his mind.

High-minded morality is reserved for high society, Dexter would often say, those who write the laws for others to obey. Anyone who says they'd never lie has never needed the grace of a fable to raise their social status. Anyone who says they'd never steal has never known the desperation of true hunger. Anyone who says they'd never kill has never had everything they love and hold dear threatened with extinction.

Olivier had rationalized the poisoning as a sort of prank, not entirely unlike the time that Fritz shoved him into the Seine on one of their wine-drunk nights with their classmates. Or the time he smeared mascara on the rim of the Celestron C8 eyepiece in the school observatory right before Olivier's mid-term presentation on the Great Pegasus Cluster. Or when Fritz had convinced him that arschgeige was a term of endearment, which almost got him clocked by a barman in Cologne. Or the one and only time that Olivier ever invited Fritz to a meditation retreat, and he spent the whole time flatulating and laughing, much to the delight, oddly enough, of the Zen master.

Olivier had measured the dose knowing Fritz's approximate body weight and thus the approximate effect. Although now thinking about, his friend did seem like he'd lost some weight in his old age. Not his usual husky build, that's for sure. Regardless, it was such a small amount it wouldn't do much more than give him a horrible headache, fever sweats… and possibly the temporary paralysis of his limbs. He simply wanted Fritz to suffer. This man to whom life had always been a golden chalice from which to drink the sweet ambrosia of innocence and mirth. Untouched by tragedy, poverty, common ills like paying rent and wondering if life was just a series of trials, tribulations, and disappointments. The privileged son of a Nobel Prize-winning chemist whose greatest rebellion was choosing, against his father's wishes, the infinite mystery of the cosmos over the inner life of a molecule.

He wanted Fritz for one night in his whole blessed life to claw at death's door and curse the day he was born. If it went too far, Olivier would rush in as the savior with the handy bottle of antivenom in his rucksack. No harm done. He even went so far as to imagine staging the heroic killing of the black scorpion, secretly letting it loose at the campfire and smashing it in front of a captive audience. So fearless, so brave. The monster vanquished, the day saved with Vera swooning into his embrace. It was a pleasant fantasy.

All he needed was the conviction to do it. He searched the sky for guidance from above. He gazed out through the telescope and roamed. He passed through

Cygnus, the Northern Cross, veering northeast until he located Vega, crystalline and gleaming. For some reason, he couldn't find Beta Lyrae, the constellation muddied by nebula and globular clusters. Perseus's famous binaries Mirfak and Angol were present though, vivid and quavering in anticipation. He traced the yin-yang medallion under his linen shirt, watching the twin stars pulse in the darkness. Yin to yang. Yang to yin. The balance of the universe. He was simply taking matters into his own hands. A karmic correction. He placed the vial in his jacket pocket and went off to join the others.

By the time he descended, a small city of tents had been raised with a roaring campfire at its center. The astronomers were settled on pillows by the flames. The nomad in the blue kaftan was nestled in the sand, cross-legged with a ginbri in his lap. He absently plucked the strings and softly sung an old Berber melody to himself. Fritz and Vera were snuggled on a blanket, listening to the sweet serenade under the dusted starlight. Olivier seated himself beside them.

Opposite him in the circle, Amadou sat on a crate. He flicked his jackknife, peeling and chopping carrots, onions, yams for the stew. Youssef tended to an iron pot cantilevered over the fire that was burbling a song of its own.

"Do you think our friend knows any singalongs?" Saul asked.

"Well, if you spoke any Arabic, you could ask him," Ingrid said.

"Why don't they speak French anymore?" Allister complained. "Arabic is such coarse language."

The nomad lifted his head from the guitar and spat

across the campfire. The spittle sizzled on the hot sand. Allister looked over, horrified. The nomad grinned. He transitioned from his beautiful Berber melody, a song as ancient as the dunes, into "Norwegian Wood" by the Beatles. The astronomers clapped.

Youssef stood dangerously close to the flames. He tore off hunks of raw meat from the goat head into the pot, already sizzling with vegetables and a thousand spices that carried their scent in the night breeze.

"What do you think, Moussa?" Fritz asked with a dumb grin, showing off his astrolabe in the firelight.

"It's a fake," Allister said.

"Quiet, he's the expert. Not you."

Moussa held the astrolabe in his palm, studying its odd markings and concentric dials. "I don't know this. What is it?"

"It's an ancient instrument that the Arabian people once used to track the stars," Fritz told him. "Some of the greatest astronomers were from North Africa and the Middle East. They were the first to discover the earth was round, track comets, predict solar eclipses, looking up at the stars from a desert much like this."

Moussa nodded, politely listening to a lecture he'd been given by countless guests at the Port d'Etoile as if it weren't the history of his own people. He showed Amadou the astrolabe. He whispered aside in Arabic. The nomad, glancing up from the melodic trance of his magic fingers, saw the artifact. His eyes narrowed. He put down his ginbri and got up to feed the camels.

Youssef reached over the campfire and sunk a ladle in the stew. He held the steam to his nose for a long time. The stew never touched his lips. Instead, he seemed to savor the taste, test the complexity of its flavors through his olfactory. Maybe his whiskers had taste buds, Olivier thought. The grey hairs winging from his nostrils did seem to have life of their own.

Youssef slopped some stew in a clay bowl, tore some bread from a loaf, and handed them off to Amadou who passed them to Saul who offered them to Allister, and so on around the circle. It was no accident that Olivier had positioned himself as the last person between Fritz and his supper. He stared into the fire, spellbound by flame. His fingers did the work in secret, uncapping the vial in his pocket. Vera was on the other side of her husband, nestled against his shoulder. Fritz kissed her on the forehead and ran his fingers through her hair.

Allister handed over another bowl. Olivier passed it down the line without looking to avoid the insufferable arrogance of Fritz's eyes. The crown prince of academia supping with his prestigious lords and ladies, his best friend who'd sunk a dagger deep in his heart and seemed to take pleasure in twisting the blade. There was a flash of orange fur behind Youssef as he dipped his ladle again into the burbling iron pot. A faint sound of claws scratching plastic. Olivier cleared his throat. The scratching stopped. Tiku surfaced in the firelight, dipping in and out of the dark, skulking behind the astronomers. Olivier passed the next bowl around the circle. Fritz handed it over to Vera.

Olivier watched and waited. Youssef scooped the goat-head stew into a bowl, steam rising like demon breath from the pits of hell. A strange smirk on their host's face. As if he knew. Olivier cupped the vial in his palm. It was so simple. He would take the bowl in his left hand, then pass it to his right hand, and in the motion, let the venom drip into the stew. He felt something brush across his lower back. Tiku pawed there, digging in the sand. Olivier shooed her away with his elbow. She scampered off and vanished into the night.

Allister passed him the bowl. It seemed hotter than the others, its clay fiery on touch. Olivier took it, deftly tipping the vial pinched in the crook of his thumb. He cradled the bowl, the stew hissing as he turned and offered it to Fritz like a gift to a king.

"Oh, you can have that one, Ollie," Fritz said. "Vera and I can share. I see how hungry you are, gazing into that bowl like it holds the answers to the nature of existence."

The astronomers chuckled with the fire. Olivier spooned the stew, pretending to eat, and smiled as if he wasn't deeply insulted.

*

AFTER a few imaginary bites and a feigned excuse of a belly ache, Olivier left the campfire, returning to his outpost on the dune so he could sulk under the stars. His nerves were jangled. He felt humiliated, overwhelmed by a deep sense of shame. He had desperately hoped that Tiku would be there waiting for him on the dune. The tuna can glistened out in the sand, barely touched. Olivier whistled. Once, twice. She would come. She always came back. There were days spent at Port d'Etoile where he wouldn't see her at all, off on her own adventures out in the Tinfu Dunes, chasing sparrows on the roof or snakes and beetles in the riad's dusty cellar.

Always, like clockwork, she would return for supper at his whistle. He sat and waited, but she was nowhere to be seen. And so, he had no one to calm his simmering anger as his shame turned to rage, as he unlatched the black case and unearthed the black scorpion.

A wiser man would have accepted his failure and reflected on the turn of events as a chance to rethink their decisions. A sign from the universe that maybe a revenge poisoning in the Sahara, hundreds of kilometers away from any doctor or medical facility, wasn't the smartest idea. This thought crossed Olivier's mind and swiftly exited.

He sunk the mason jar in the sand. The black scorpion thrashed its tail while he strapped on rubber gloves. Its stinger pinged the glass with such force that he truly feared it might crack. From under the foam padding, he collected the instruments needed for the milking, which he'd brought in case the vial broke in transit—a pair of hookah tongs, a nine-volt battery, a syringe. He unspooled a bolt of copper wire, looping it several times around the tong handle as Amadou had done, then proceeded to connect the positive and negative ends to the battery terminals. He felt a light buzz through the metal—electricity coursing through, electrons excited by their freedom. This delighted him, its sorcery, this power rushing from the activated acid and lead of the battery cell through his own cells. He pinched the tongs together, shooting sparks into the night.

The lid was stubborn, his hands unsteady. He gripped it firmly and wrenched, wary that the instant the jar was opened, the black scorpion might lunge out in vengeance for its captivity. Strangely, the ancient assassin had stilled, as if waiting for its release. The lid popped open. He set the jar in the sand. The scorpion made a half-hearted attempt to climb up the smooth glass, failing and trying again. Then it lay docile, cowed by the enormous shadow of its captor. Or so Olivier assumed. He crouched, face to face with the monster, and reached toward the jar. At the sight of the tongs, the scorpion skittered in a frenzy, rocking the glass prison until it tipped.

Olivier scrambled away. The scorpion crawled out onto the sand, its stinger primed. He hunched and stared the monster down, tongs outstretched, readying himself like a bullfighter. The scorpion circled once, twice, then rushed at his feet. He waited for the precise moment it was within reach and clasped its curled tail.

The scorpion convulsed in shock, its spindly legs peddling the air, the tongs clamped on its black armor, electricity exciting beads of venom from the thorn. Olivier raised the syringe to siphon them from its stinger. His grip was so shaky that he failed again and again, knocking off the milky drops. He tried to steady his hand, but his whole body was juddering with nervousness and the electrical charge of the nine-volt battery, his energy connected with the poor creature being tortured. Then it stopped. Both his own trembling and that of the scorpion. Nothing more came from its thorn.

He let go of the newly dead scorpion—soon to be very dead scorpion—and tried to convince himself it was still alive. That it was sleeping, or playing dead, or in a catatonic state of shock. The ancient assassin remained immobile, its legs stiff. He prodded it with the tongs, attempting to goad it back to life. Crestfallen, Olivier refused to believe his plan had failed again. There must be venom inside the tail, he reasoned. Perhaps he could find way, some sinew in the joint of its armor where he could plunge the syringe and extract it.

A bobbing light rose up the slope from the campfire. Olivier disconnected the battery and stuffed the instruments into his rucksack. He then dug a hole and lightly covered the scorpion with sand. He pretended to busy himself with the Criterion Dynascope.

His old friend summited the dune, holding an oil lantern.

"How goes it, Ollie?" Fritz said. "I brought some light in case you need it."

"I managed in the dark just fine," he said, peering into the telescope. "Snuff that out, will you? You're ruining my night vision."

"Alright then. No need to get huffy. Just trying to help." Fritz placed the lantern down and stood over the telescope. "Mind if I have a look?"

Olivier felt his body seize and stiffen. An innocent request, perhaps, except for the way Fritz said it, like the way he said most everything, this low-throated arrogance, grainy in his voice as if he was trying hide it. A self-certain entitlement, a resentment for having to ask permission at all instead of just bopping him on the head like a neanderthal and shoving him aside.

Olivier stepped away from the telescope and rose. Fritz stood there, a foot taller than him, still wearing his ridiculous headscarf, even though the threat of the sun was long gone. Olivier searched for his old friend's eyes in the cloth, their gleam in the starlight, for something, anything to abate this wrathful tide that welled inside of him, ready to sweep out into dunes.

Fritz smirked, somehow misinterpreting Olivier's stonewall grimace for affection. He kneeled beside the telescope and started fiddling with the knobs.

"Ah, fantastic," he said. "Let's see if we can find M102."

The lantern glowed on the sand, its flame flickering with banded rays of soft light, barely escaping the glass, overpowered by the vast darkness of the dunes and eternal abyss of space above.

"Where are you, Draconis?" Fritz asked the stars. "It should be there."

"Aren't you going to put it out?"

"Huh?"

"The lantern," Olivier said. "I asked you to snuff it out."

Fritz removed his eye from the viewfinder and made a sour face.

"Oh, well, we might need it," he said and returned to the telescope. "But if it really bothers you, go right ahead. Maybe these old eyes are better than yours, but the light has no effect on what I'm seeing here."

Standing only a few feet from the buried scorpion, Olivier sensed a disturbance in the sand. Or perhaps it was only fantasy. Perhaps it was his fierce untamable anger that quaked the desert, awaking the spirit of its monsters. Fritz, oblivious as usual, was on his knees, jerking the telescope toward quadrants of the night sky, the bare heels of his sandaled feet swaying as if to a song in his head.

The sand trembled again. The bell tolled in the

tower of Olivier's mind, not its usual deep tone but a shrill piercing ring. The yin-yang medallion icy against his heaving chest. He reached down into the shallow grave and snatched the dead scorpion. He squeezed its stinger, watching beads sweat on its slick thorn. He blew out the lantern.

"Ah, the Pleiades are looking gorgeous tonight," Fritz said. "This brings me back. I love this telescope, Ollie. It feels so… real, you know? True starlight, no filter, no digital noise, reaching back from millions of years to us. It's so old school, I mean, kind of like you. No offense, of course. OUCH! DAMN IT!"

Fritz yowled and clutched his foot, toppling backward in an overly melodramatic fall.

"Did you see it, Ollie? Something bit me."

"Maybe it's just your imagination."

"Imagination?" Fritz said. "My foot is bleeding."

"Is it? Hmm, I can't see," Olivier said. "Where's that lantern?"

"Ooh, it burns, it burns, it BURNS! What the hell? What was it?"

"Could be a lizard."

"They have teeth?"

"Oh yes, they are quite vicious out here. Let's have a look."

Olivier sat down. Fritz stretched out his leg and surrendered his heel onto his friend's lap. Olivier almost felt sorry for him, a savage kind of pity. Fritz sweating in the dark, consumed by wild fears. The distinguished scientist reduced to this whining child. Olivier explored the contours of his heel until he found the tiny wound. It was only a pinprick, a little ragged at the edges, skin torn and puckered.

"Definitely a lizard."

"Ouch, that hurts."

"What hurts? I'm not doing anything."

Fritz's whimpering soon attracted the attention of the astronomers around campfire. Allister and Ingrid trudged up the dune to investigate. Stay or go, stay or go. The moment of decision had come, Olivier had met it with conviction. However, without any controlling variables, he had no idea what to expect. How much poison had the stinger delivered? Was it less or more than the dose he'd calculated?

Olivier crushed the scorpion in his fist and let its crumbled exoskeleton fall behind him, discreetly burying the servant of death with a sweep of his hand, soon to be rendered anonymous, black flecks of chitlin and calcium carbonate, lost in the vast expanse of particle matter, of sand, of nothingness.

"Everything okay?" Ingrid asked.

Fritz swung his tender foot from Olivier's lap. "Of course! Come, stay, it's all set up." He hunched over the telescope. "We may be in luck for one of your favorites, Ingrid. The archer is out shooting tonight."

"Don't be a tease." Ingrid passed over a bottle of wine. "Let me see, Fritz."

Olivier stood in silent observation, perplexed. If in fact the stinger had delivered the venom through the hard callous of his heel, the neurotoxins in his blood should have been enflaming his nerves with an excruciating pain, swelling his foot, ankle, tendons. If this were true, Fritz was somehow suppressing this intense pain, impressively so. But why? For the sake of civility? Out of pride? After all, he was the undisputed leader of the pack. To show vulnerability was to admit weakness. It did not matter that these were academics. Maybe this made the instinctual competition for top dog even worse, given the complex hierarchical structures of academic institutions. Maybe he was pretending not to feel anything to protect his fragile masculinity. Fritz glugged some wine, burped, and toyed with the focus ring on the telescope. Or maybe he was just drunk.

"Where's the astrolabe?" Allister asked.

"Oh, now you're interested in my astrolabe," Fritz said.

"May I see it?"

"Sure, if you admit that it isn't a fake." Fritz said, handing over the astrolabe.

Allister played with the brass plates of the mater. "As a scientist, I will remain open-minded to the remote possibility that the astrolabe you bought for the price of a cheap watch is really a centuries-old heirloom that once belonged to the king of a Tuareg tribe…" He aligned the rete with the desert stars overhead, trying to determine latitude and longitude. "…in the same way that I hold open the possibility that light could ever escape a black hole, or that stars have a willful life of their own."

Allister smirked sharply. Fritz and Ingrid bawled with laughter. Olivier grabbed his rucksack and stormed off, wishing he had enough poison to kill them all.

He stumbled down the dune toward the campfire. Instead of guilt or remorse, he was overcome by a familiar existential dread, a hopelessness weighted by his failures. Had he really so utterly and completely fumbled his revenge? No, Fritz would suffer soon enough, he comforted himself. Who knows he could die? He looked back, overcome with a pang of regret. The astronomers were laughing and rough housing on top of the dune. Poisons work slowly, he reassured himself. Perhaps he'd been poisoned too during his botched attempt to milk the scorpion. It was a risk. For some reason, this didn't bother him. Some part of him knew that he'd been waiting, wanting to die for years, out in the lonesome Draa Valley.

The rest of the traveling party was slumped around the campfire in post-prandial bliss, sleepily listening to the magical guitar of the nomad in the blue kaftan. Amadou was nodding off on a crate. Saul had passed out in the sand. Even Moussa seemed relaxed and perfectly content, laid out on his back, eyes closed, smiling up at the night sky.

Olivier walked through camp on the lookout for Tiku. He inspected the refuse pile near the iron pot where the goat-head carcass had been discarded along with vegetable roots and peels. He discovered a light trail of paw prints and followed their circuitous path through the sand.

"Ollie, you alright?" Vera asked. She hovered over him, haloed by the warm glow of the campfire. He wanted her to go away. He struggled to look at her. Her eyes, their colors seemingly alive, swirling, penetrative.

"Yes, I'm fine," he said and continued following the tracks.

"You don't seem fine."

He could not handle her sweetness. He felt so fragile that he might crumble to dust if she dared touch him. She came closer. He ignored her, analyzing the desert's fine grain, the confusing map of intersecting paw prints, where tracks converged, where a new set began again in a different direction.

"Ollie, seriously, what's going on? You're shaking. Are you sick?"

Olivier avoided her interrogative gaze, feeling queasy. He wiped the sweat from his hot forehead. Perhaps the poison did work after all. Perhaps too well.

"Ollie…"

"Leave me alone. I need to find Tiku."

Vera laughed. "Your cat?"

"It's not funny," he said. "She's lost."

"I'm sorry, yes, I can see that. It's just that you brought your cat out to the Sahara."

"She's not my cat," Olivier said. "She's feral, born in the desert. I'm sure she's okay. I'm just concerned because she didn't eat her supper. Now if you'll excuse me…"

Deciding on a set of tracks at random, Olivier wandered off away from camp to find his lost cat. Or perish in the dunes. Or perhaps both.

9.

THE dunes seemed an endless climb into the starry dynamo. Trudging up the slopes, sand cascading underfoot, Olivier followed the paw prints into the night along the ridges, swerves, and finback crests. From the highest peak, three ranges out from camp, he peered over the vast dunescape and searched the pooled darkness in the valleys for any scurrying. The stars shone bright in the fishbowl, the nebulous mist of the Milky Way banding across the firmament, the desert luminant with an eerie indigo. Still no Tiku. Only faint trails leading farther into the expanse of sand.

Dune after dune, he laid bare his hopes, desperate to find his furry companion, miraculously discovering more impressions in the sand whenever he was sure he'd lost the trail. He chided himself for bringing Tiku, for agreeing to this idiotic excursion, for his foolish scheme of revenge. The uncertainty of his friend's fate was a certain kind of madness. Fritz was either reveling under the stars or writhing in agony. A Schrodinger's

Cat paradox, he laughed to himself. He wouldn't know until he returned. And what would happen then? There was no way of determining how much poison he'd delivered or whether he'd delivered any at all. What if he'd accidentally killed his old friend? Blood pounded in his ears, his heartbeat like a drum that echoed inside his head, out into the desert, underneath the sand. And what about Vera? She knew he'd done something terrible. An absurd thought. Not entirely rational. She had a funny way of always uncovering the truth in his eyes. He stood alone with these thoughts and the universe in the clear night over the Sahara, alone in the tower of his mind, a familiar place—his sanctuary—disturbed by a nagging guilt as he ruminated on whether to turn back or continue onward.

Summiting the next dune, same as the last, same as forever, he whistled and called out for Tiku, her name rolling into the undulating darkness, over the emptiness, this borderland of nowhere, this no man's land between Morocco and Algeria. He listened for her soft meow somewhere out there in the night. The echo deadened, the desert silent. Over the crest, her tiny paw prints faded away into smooth windswept sand. He inspected the last claw marks, speculating on a direction. If he continued straight, maybe he would rediscover her trail beyond the next ridge. Or perhaps Tiku had turned around. Maybe she'd realized she'd gone too far.

He looked skyward and hunted for Beta Lyrae, locating the Harp without much trouble this time. Sheliak danced in the stardust of Lyra. Albireo shone fierce in the head of Cygnus. However, it was Mirfak again that caught his attention, shimmering north of the Seven Sisters. The variable star seemingly pulsed brighter and brighter, shining from a hundred parsecs away in its lonely coordinates in the infinitude of space. He exhaled out into the desert, up to the atmosphere, unaware he'd been holding his breath.

He remembered the first time he'd seen it as a young boy. After his parents had gone to bed, he'd snuck out of his bedroom, up to the attic and through the skylight onto the shingled roof, alone with the universe, a celestial playground to explore for hours with his telescope. He'd been amazed by its vibrant sparkle, searching his book of star charts for its name. Alpha Persei, also known as Mirfak. An ancient and sacred name. As a child lost in the starlight, it felt as if it shined just for him. So brilliant, so vivacious in its radiance. All his dreams, all his hopes. His heart full, alive in the stars.

The beginning of a foolish theory, he thought. How could stars have a life of their own? They were only hydrogen and helium. Gaseous cores shedding atomic wildfire and stellar wind in the deep void of space. And yet gazing up into the jeweled sky, he didn't quite believe this either.

He scooped up a handful of sand and let the fine grains sift through his fingers. What ever happened to that curious boy—his blissful wonder, his faith in the stars? How had he become such so cynical, so mistrustful, so fearful? Time marches on, he thought, and we have no choice but to follow. Entropy, the only true law of the universe, a natural corruption. We are born, we age, we die. Vera understood this from her timeless vantage point as an astrophysicist. Her energy exuded a reverent gratitude for the present moment, resonant with the history of all things, the kinetic potential of all things. He missed the exhilaration of feeling alive in her presence. No longer a disembodied mind but a man with a beating heart. Breathing in atmosphere, feeling the oxygen enrich the cells of his being.

How much of his life had he spent alone, contemplating the mysteries of the cosmos coded in the stars? Existing somewhere between here and there, floating through life in a liminal space between the theoretical and actual, the imagined and the real, his mind analyzing all horizons, steering between all possible pasts, all possible futures, detached from the anchored present of his body, the earth, the soil and sand. He had not cared until he met her. He'd been content to live out his days as a radical philosopher of the stars, in exile for his heretical beliefs. And then the supernova of her eyes had set off a chain reaction of explosions, implosions, and formations that altered his orbit forever, drawn toward those thousand suns in her gaze, the light of which seemed to dispel dark matter from the deepest parts of himself.

The night air held a chill, the sand cool on touch, soothing since his whole body felt so flush and hot. His thoughts turned again to Fritz. He imagined his old friend sobered by brutal pain and misery as the venom coursed through his veins and hijacked his nervous system. What have I done? Olivier thought. Could he really blame Fritz for falling for her? It seemed so easy to do. Fritz didn't deserve to die out in the desert, even if he was a pompous ignoramus, blithely marching through life in his own self-important bubble. A goofy, lovable, sweet buffoon with a heart as big as his numbskull head.

Olivier rose and brushed off his knees. Maybe there was still time. The antivenom. Yes, he could deliver the antidote. Make amends and maybe a few excuses. Nobody needed to know the whole truth. In the tail of the Great Bear, he aligned with Polaris, captain's friend, the compass point glowing bright in the mythic sky. He tried to visualize the coordinates of the starry sky over camp. The north star had been visible over the dune where he'd set up the telescope, he remembered. Slightly to the right. Which meant he must have walked northeast. So if he headed southwest, he would eventually find camp.

Guided by the north star and his own faded sandal prints, he began his pilgrimage back to camp. He hurriedly retraced his steps, hiking the gigantic dunes, trekking along the fins, his feet sinking deep into the scratchy sand. Somewhere between the fourth and fifth range, his sandal prints vanished without a trace in the shifting desert. Despite this, he maintained the faith that he would see something, anything over the next ridge besides more sand.

The night grew colder, his feet grew tired, and for some reason, his fingertips burned. A slow cloud drift began to obscure the edges of the northern sky, seeping like smoke over the stars. Thin clouds crept in, closing the veil. He raced up a steep slope, slipping, falling, finally gaining traction. By the time he reached its peak, there was no north star to be found. Only a vast muddy greyness that melded into the shadowed dunes. The jester of the universe was taunting him. He did not find it funny. He cursed the clouds, the desert, the stupid stars, his stupid heart, all his foolish ambitions, his cowardice, his mistakes, too proud to ever compromise.

His mentor Wolfgang Hume had warned him years ago at the Sorbonne. "Your pride will be your downfall," he'd said. "It is an honorable thing to hold fast to your beliefs, but we are scientists. We deal in science. Empirical, analytic truth. Not metaphysics. You think you are smarter than everyone. You are so convinced of your own genius that you do not listen to good council. But please listen to me now. You are not smarter. You may hold a brilliance within you, but you lack discipline. Listen to me, Olivier. You can push the margins of science, but if you want to be an iconoclast, you will never make it in academia."

He had recommended that Olivier change his doctoral thesis to focus on a wide range of theories about why his so-called "rebel stars" exhibited unusual behavior. Perhaps he could include an addendum supposition on stars having a "willful energy", but no one would allow it to be part of his main argument. That was absurd. Olivier felt angry, remembering those words, how they wounded him for years. They hurt because he knew that Wolfgang was right.

He gazed out over the dark Sahara, the mountainous dunes casting out for miles and miles. It was then that he realized it was too late. Fear gripped his heart. A paralyzing sense of total ruin. He was indeed lost in the great unfathomable desert amid the great unfathomable darkness.

The bell tolled again in his mind, as he stood there in the dunes, isolated in time and space, as if the exact moment had been predetermined by some cosmic fate. Perhaps predestined from his first step onto a bus headed out from Marrakesh through the sinuous roads of the Atlas Mountains into the Draa Valley. Had he travelled so far in search of answers and a new beginning, all those years ago, for this? Oh, the great irony of settling down in the desert, as if he could expect to grow roots somewhere where nothing grew but boredom and the shadow of death.

His body alternated flush to cold, certain that he too had been poisoned. He waited for his limbs to stiffen, his heart to seize. Was this really the end? An anonymous death in the desert, never to be found, with not even the stars for company. What did it matter? Who cared who died, who lived, who loved? Who triumphed, who failed, who survived? We invent meaning to give our pathetic little lives purpose, he thought. We are nothing more than minnows in the great rushing river of time, wriggling bacteria in the cosmic gut, parasitic specks of life in an insignificant galaxy in an immeasurable unforgiving universe. In the end, all our hopes, passions, dreams, everything we hold dear will become nothing more than dust. None of it mattered. He repeated this to himself, he knew it as empirical truth, but he did not want to believe it. The emptiness for too long had felt like home.

All he wanted—all he prayed for from the jester, goddesses, or impartial stardust—was to hear Tiku's innocent meow once again. He wanted to feel her furry warmth nuzzled against him as she did many nights at the Port d'Etoile, pawing his chest to see if he was awake. He needed her then, more than he'd ever needed anything or anyone. He needed her to scurry up his leg and lower back, onto his shoulders, trusting him as if he were worthy of her love.

All his life he'd thought he'd never needed anyone. He was self-sufficient. Smart, capable, cunning. He was only fooling himself. Life needs life, he thought. Life feeds life. An accelerant tessellation. We are symbiotic beings that cannot be removed from the ecosystem. Yes, the thrill of adventure, discovery, recognition had driven his pursuits, but it was the constellation of people he'd met over the years that fueled him. The nights with Pascal on the hills at Mount Wilson, stoned and laughing with stars. Potluck dinners with the motley crew of international scientists at Cerro Tololo in Chile. His university escapades with Fritz. His quests with Vera to witness the night-sky wonders of the world. Even the quiet mornings with annoying Moussa sipping tea out in the courtyard while the desert sun rose over the Tinfu Dunes.

It was in these shared moments with others that he truly felt alive. There was no escaping nor denying the compounding effect of these links, orbits, accretions in the constellation of life. And what was love except a connection so powerful that its thermodynamic transference rendered you changed? Something so true and necessary when it was looking you in the eyes or licking your face with its sandpaper tongue. Something so painful when it was gone, the memory of love we call grief in all its many forms.

He searched the cloud scrim for any constellations, any connection between the glimmery smudges in the grey veil. The night wind breezed through his bushy hair. He told himself to be patient. Clouds move, the darkness will pass, the stars will show themselves again.

It was then that he saw something move in the distance, a shadow crawling across the shadows, ever so faint. He rubbed clean his glasses and strained his eyes.

"Tiku!" he called out. "Tiku, is that you?"

The shadow dipped in and out of view, trekking its way across a far-off dune.

"Don't run away, you rascal," Olivier shouted. "Tiku! I'm sorry!"

The movement ceased. Stillness reigned and he worried he'd lost the lively shadow. And then it showed itself again, climbing a dune.

"Ollie?"

The cat had somehow—magic of the Sahara, bizarre energy vortex of the desert—gained a voice. How strange and how wonderful, he thought.

"Tiku!" he called out.

"Ollie!" the voice cried out. The shadow grew taller, up and over the dune, guided by a flickering orb that seemed to hover over it. The shadow and its mystical sprite bobbed through the dark, floating along the ridge, crossing to where Olivier stood in amazement.

"Ollie, it's me," Vera said, holding up the lantern to her face.

"It is you," Olivier replied. She'd come searching for him. His heart swelled so full he could feel it beat in his throat. His whole body quaked, his mind blinked. Did she know? Had Moussa sent her? Was this some ruse to lure him back to camp so he could face justice?

"Oh, thank god you're alright." She placed the lantern in the sand and threw her arms around him.

Olivier struggled to breathe, his thoughts racing. Was he being rewarded for his crimes? What clever trick was the jester playing on him?

"We were so worried," she said.

"We?" Olivier asked.

"Well, you know, Fritz and the others…"

"Oh, I'm surprised they noticed I was gone."

"Okay, smartass, I was worried," she said, pulling away. "Why do you have to be such a jerk about it? I've been searching for you across the goddamn desert for almost an hour."

"Sorry… I still haven't found Tiku."

"Maybe she's wandered back by now. Oof, I'm so tired."

Vera sat down on the dune and began to unlace her boots. Olivier followed her lead, sitting beside her. Starlight gleamed through the thin clouds, the grey veil slowly dissipating like mist.

Vera dumped out sand from her boots. "This desert is almost as exhausting to walk as it is look at."

"You don't find it enchanting?" Olivier joked, gesturing out to the nothingness. "The marvelous Sahara."

"It reminds me of Mauna Kea in weird way. The shape of the dunes, you know? They're kind of like volcano craters."

"Hmm, I can see that. I'd forgotten about that trip."

"Another lifetime." Vera stripped off her socks and wiggled her toes.

Mauna Kea had been their last trip together. Spring of 1998, shortly before Olivier had become the resident astronomer at the Port d'Etoile. Vera was on break from Oxford where she was finishing her doctorate in astrophysics. Olivier had just returned from a six-month stint as a tour guide for an ancient astronomy trek in Turkey, which was half fact, half fiction with scientists like himself expounding on the knowledge and tools transferred along the Silk Road while esteemed crackpots held lectures about extraterrestrial visits and the possibility that this otherworldly wisdom came from outer space.

Once again, Vera and Olivier had traded letters and phone calls but hadn't seen each other in over a year. And so, they decided to go to see Mauna Kea together, the sacred volcano on Big Island that had become an international outpost with dozens of observatories erected on the summit by different nations—United States, Canada, China, France, Japan. Olivier knew a junior data analyst working at the Caltech Submillimeter Array. Vera had a friend of friend who was stationed at the Gemini North observatory. They'd arrived without much of a plan.

What followed was one catastrophe after another, cranking up the dirt road toward the summit in a banged-up jeep with shocks so worn that it felt like it was held together by pixie sticks and bubblegum. First, Olivier became ill from altitude sickness. Second, his friend had greatly exaggerated his clout at the Caltech Submillimeter Array and they were swiftly kicked out after a brief tour of the observation deck. Then the jeep had predictably tipped into a roadside ditch on the way up to Gemini North.

They'd spent hours trying to wave down every utility vehicle that passed, waiting for someone to help haul them out. The sun went down without any luck. The volcano lit up with a surreal fire and settled into an unreal haze, fading out to pure night as the immense starlight faded in out of nowhere. They slept in the jeep that night, side by side like teenagers.

Olivier remembered waking to the weight of her body draped over him. It surprised him. Her head on his chest, her hand over his heart. He stayed awake the rest of the night, daring not to move and disturb this heaven on earth. The next morning, they'd lucked out with a tow from a maintenance truck and decided to spend the rest of their stay in a thatched roof hut on the coast.

"What a disaster," Vera said.

"Ah, come on, we still made the best of it," Olivier said. "We had a couple days of paradise on the beach."

"Oh Waipi'o… that was a dream."

"We should have never come back."

Vera uncapped her canteen and tried to coax the last drops in her mouth. She asked if he had any water.

"Sadly no, but ah hold on, I may have something…" Olivier searched inside his rucksack and pulled out a tall boy of Köstritzer. "Want some?"

"Sure, why not?" she said.

"Cheers." He cracked open the tall boy, foam bubbling over, wet rivulets fizzing down the slope. They shared the beer together on the dune. The clouds had cleared away, the theater of stars majestic in the desert sky for them and them alone, or so it felt out there, lost in the Sahara.

"Like old times," Vera said. "I've missed you, Ollie."

"I've missed you too," Olivier said.

"Then why haven't you called? Why haven't you come to visit? I know things are weird between you and Fritz…"

"Oh, don't. Please."

"He worries about you, too."

"Does he?" Olivier said. The beer tasted bitter. His guilty conscience returned with its circus of ruminations. He's fine, Olivier reassured himself. She wouldn't have come looking for him if her husband were delirious, suffering the fire of the scorpion's sting. Of course, there was a chance, always a chance in our reality of probabilities, that she'd gone out searching for him before Fritz had shown any symptoms. A disturbing thought he didn't want to deal with at the moment. He dismissed it and drank more beer.

"Are you going to spend the rest of your life in the desert?" she asked. "Seriously. Come home, come back to Europe."

"There's nothing for me there," he said.

"There's civilization. There's something other than sand!"

"I like sand."

"No, you don't," she said. "You always used to complain whenever we'd camp out on the beach. Oh, the sand is so hot. Oh, I don't like the way it feels on my feet. I'm gonna get a sunburn. I prefer my leisure time less itchy."

Olivier gulped down some beer. "People change."

"Do they?" she said. "I've been beginning to wonder that myself. The way you and Fritz behave together it's like you're stuck as schoolyard rivals forever."

"I've made my life here and I'm very content."

"You're a terrible liar, Ollie. I've never seen you so miserable. I can't just stand by and watch you waste away in the desert. It's like you've given up on life entirely."

"And what if I have? What does it matter, Vera? We're all going to die someday and carry our meaningless regrets to the grave."

"We are here, Ollie. We are alive. Look up there and tell me what you see."

Olivier glanced up at the stars. "Light, heat, gas. A pretty illusion that's really just mayhem."

"How pleasant," Vera said. "What happened to Ollie the dreamer? Remember that night in Iceland on our second trip together?"

"It was brutally cold. I had trouble sleeping, I remember that."

"We'd just seen the Northern Lights and you said something about how we're connected to it, all of it, the electromagnetic continuity of the universe, in an invisible web spiraling through space and time. It was an empirical fact, you said. Just look at the outer crust of neutron stars and how it resembles our own cellular membranes. We are energy in the form of matter. Concentrations of energy. Born of the cosmos, progeny of stardust, that's what you said. Iron in our blood, phosphorous in our DNA—"

"I was probably high."

"You know what I see?" Vera said, looking out at the desert sky. "I see a miracle. What began with a brilliant flash, matter and antimatter annihilating each other in a quantum game of ping pong until the slightest asymmetry let the first photons escape, forming quarks, electrons, neutrons, protons, nucleuses. Nebulas, stars, galaxies—"

"Just like a wind-up toy," Olivier said.

"This place, Earth, our goldilocks home in perfect orbit around the sun—"

"A lucky accident."

"Does that make it any less amazing? The serendipity of life, the evolution of all the curious little creatures competing for survival. The astounding phenomenon of human consciousness, the rapid genesis of languages, ideas, civilization." Vera raised her beer in honor of the stars. "We are witnesses of the miracle. What difference does our judgment of it make? The fact that we even have the cognitive power to question existence… that's significant, that's miraculous, that matters."

"I guess," Olivier said. "But isn't it also depressing? These enormous questions that will never be answered? I feel like I've wasted my whole life trying to decode mysteries in the night sky. And for what? It seems pointless considering what I gave up in my idiotic quest to prove the impossible. I feel like a fool."

"Why?"

"Because I lost you."

The words thudded like stones in the sand. For a moment, it felt as if the Sahara rippled, dunes changing shape under the starlight. Vera became very quiet. She reached over and rested her hand on his knee.

"Ollie, I'm right here," she said.

At first, he couldn't face her. He dammed his eyes closed to stem any leakage. His heart raced fast, as if it had been empty and quite suddenly pumped full of blood, thrumming. Then he rested his hand on top of hers and gazed into her eyes, lost in their nebulous layers.

"The happiest moments of my life have been with you," Olivier said.

She didn't break eye contact. She didn't shy away. She wasn't afraid. She was never afraid. It was infuriating.

"I feel the same way," she said. "But it's complicated."

"Does it have to be?"

"Oh, Ollie, please, this is hard."

"What if we said to hell with it all and just go?" Olivier said with a burst of energy, his heart singing wild.

"Where?"

"Anywhere, everywhere. Does it matter?"

"I'm married, Ollie," she said, flashing her ring.

"So?"

"Stop it. It's not that simple."

"Isn't it?" he said. "Isn't this what the bards write about? Star-crossed lovers running away to live happily ever after."

"You do realize Romeo and Juliet kill themselves in the end?"

"Vera…" he said, searching for her eyes again.

"I love him too, Ollie," she said. "He's my person. He's my life."

Olivier kicked the sand and crumpled his arms.

"Is it so hard to believe that someone can hold many loves in their heart?" Vera asked.

"Yes, it's absurd," Olivier said. "Besides, you know, I'm much funnier and a better cook."

"I love Fritz so much it hurts." She trembled, her eyes glassy. "He's dying, Ollie. He's dying."

Olivier's mind spun. Was Fritz dying right then in a tent, spasming and sweating in a vicious fever, while they were drinking beer on a dune? If that were the case, what on earth was she doing here? He tried to summon any words that might put her at ease.

"I'm sure it's just indigestion," he said. "He'll feel better in the morning."

"Huh?" she said, wiping her tears. "He has cancer, Ollie."

Olivier swallowed hard on his beer. Vera elaborated on his condition. The late stages of pancreatic cancer. The lining of his pancreas plagued with tumorous lesions, threatening to spread into the lower intestine and liver. She relayed this in a cold frank manner, with complicated medical terms and graphic imagery of his symptoms—the headaches, nausea, violent cramps, incontinence, hair loss—before she broke down crying again.

Olivier was both moved and fascinated. He couldn't recall if he'd ever seen Vera cry before. A real cry, that is, a full sawhorse sob, wind caught in the throat, her beautiful eyes burning hot with tears. She'd witnessed Olivier's blubbering plenty of times, often over stupid trivial things—a broken watch, lost baggage, stubbing his big toe—and one time over the not-so-trivial death of his father.

"Fritz has his good days and his bad days," she said. "He's on a lot of drugs for the pain."

"Vera, that's awful," he said. "We've come so far with precision medicine and modern oncology. I'm sure there's still a chance—"

"No. Not really. It's too late," she said. "The doctor says he most likely only has a matter of months before it metastasizes to his other organs and then things get much worse. That's why we came down here. So he could say goodbye."

Olivier was speechless with no idea what to say or how to react. Oh god, what have I done? he thought. He filled the uncomfortable silence by cracking open another beer.

"Fritz acts so strong all the time, you know? I'm trying. I'm really trying..."

Vera wrapped herself around him. She buried her wet face in his shoulder. Olivier cocooned her and let her sob. He wanted to hold her forever, affixed like the twin stars of Sheliak, the Harp in its eternal dance. Would she cry like this for him, he wondered? A selfish thought. He should have been thinking about Fritz and his own idiocy. Regardless of the outcome, he would soon lose a dear friend.

No matter how hard he shunned them, selfish thoughts clouded his mind like gases congregating in a nebula, readying the birth of a star. Her breath so hot and heavy on his neck, her soft body nestled in this awkward embrace. He could feel every nerve, every cell, every molecule, every nucleus, every electron bound across space and time. It felt as if he had suddenly returned to his sad body after years of interstellar travel, her tenderness delivering this poor alien back to earth, her electromagnetic field like a pulsar that soothed and excited him, raising the temperature of his biochemical heat. In short, he was aroused, entirely inappropriate of course, as was the twirl of his fingers, curling back the long strands of hair by her ear.

"I don't know what I'm going do without him. I don't know..."

Olivier lifted her chin. Tears fell down her face, and he fell deep into her cosmic eyes. Is this wrong? he thought. Or is this right? He leaned closer. She leaned closer. Her heart aching, his heart breaking. Their breath tightened, inch by inch. Her expectant eyes luminant and tunneling, his shaky hand upon her cheek. Then she grabbed him by the collar, pressing her lips deep into his own.

Olivier had waited a lifetime for this kiss. He'd expected magic, fireworks, the wings of their birdsong unfurled together, ascending to an interdimensional plane of ecstatic consciousness. It was nothing like that. For all the love they held for each other, the kiss felt like the way she smiled at him. A playground kiss, innocent and sweet and incredibly awkward. He faulted his own lack of bravado. He doubled down on his passion. He dipped her under the stars, knocking over the beer can in the process, sand fizzling in the dark, attempting the Belgian version of a French kiss, their mouths briny and parched with the sour aftertaste of beer. His neck cricked. He broke away.

"Well, that was something," she said. "Something we should probably keep private between the two of us."

"Sorry," he said.

"I'm not," she said. "Are you?"

"No."

"Well, don't say you're sorry then," she said, tying up her boots. "We should go."

"Yes," Olivier replied. He rose from the dune, legs shaking, sand shifting, struggling to find solid footing on the spinning earth. Out and beyond, the eternity of stars wavered with a dewy lucence across the vast lumpy darkness. He gathered up his knapsack and slung it over his shoulder. He then lifted his heart from the sand, wet and gritty, finally expelled from its cage, and dusted it off.

10.

THEY traveled southwest over the dunes, guided by Polaris and the broad arrows that Vera had marked on every ridge she'd crossed so she could retrace her way back to camp. A smart idea. Why hadn't he thought of that? Olivier trailed behind her. He dreaded the judgement that awaited him. Three hours, more or less… that was the approximate window to administer the antivenom. How long had he been lost in the desert? What if Fritz was already dead? It was probable, if not likely, that even the tiniest drop of venom could cause total havoc on his compromised immune system. Olivier considered kicking off down a dune and escaping toward the boundless horizon, far, far away until he found someplace where he could lay his anxious weary body and wait for the desert to swallow him whole. Every time he came close to breaking away, she would look over her shoulder as if she knew, as if telling him to have courage and stay.

Vera summited a dune and waited for him, arms

akimbo. "Come on, Ollie. I get it, you feel guilty, but please stop flogging yourself like a monk."

He clambered up the slope and took hold of her hand. They walked together along the ridge.

"You're not the only one who's wondered," she said. "Are you mad at me?"

"Why would I be mad at you?"

"Because I fell in love with Fritz," she said. "I knew about the cancer before I married him. We'd found out shortly after we were engaged. He told me to go and be happy with someone else."

It was painful to hear her tragic love story, the way she told it with heavy pauses of silence, as if Fritz were already ten years in the grave. It was difficult to hear her grieve and admit to himself that their love was real and undeniable. He shuffled along, tethered to her as she squeezed his hand and wouldn't let go. He wasn't sure what hurt more, his sore feet in his sandals or his bruised heart ragged from its violent liberation.

"I know you don't want to hear this, but I'm so grateful," she said. "Without you, he would have never been in my life."

Olivier let go of her, his palm slippery. He hurried up the next dune, tired and clumsy. His breath shortened. His chest tightened. He felt sharp arrhythmic pangs, terrified that he might have a real heart attack out there in the stupid dunes.

"Ollie…" she called out. "Stop acting like a child."

"I know what you see in him."

"Oh, do you now? You can see through my eyes? That's a clever trick."

"You're not the first person to fall in love with that goofball."

Fritz, the jolly giant, could win anyone over with his waggish charm. What was it that Fritz had said the first time they crossed paths at the Sorbonne, that cool spring night in 1972? Oh yes—hello there, your shirt's untucked. That's what he'd said, looking up at the façade of the Chappelle. He said nothing of that fact Olivier, with his mussy hair and tweed, was hanging out on a marble ledge, some twenty feet off the ground, smoking a joint while searching the night sky with his telescope.

"What of it?" Olivier had retorted. "Do we have to be so formal all the time?"

He recognized Fritz from astronomy class—the yawning, spit-balling aristocrat who was the perfect student, a picture of civility whenever the professor's back wasn't turned. He ingratiated himself to the other students as a lovable prankster, which saved him from ridicule over the teenage acne that scarred his face.

Fritz concurred that Olivier had a fair point about the university's propriety and general fussiness, however he could see the stripes of his underwear. He then asked the obvious question: what was he doing up a ledge in the middle of the night? Olivier told him that he was trying to observe the radial velocity of Albireo.

"They lock up the damn building after 9pm," Olivier had said. "It's nonsensical. We're supposed to be night owls. What else are we to do? There's no way up to the tower, no way into the observatory—"

"Unless you have a key." Fritz smirked, drawing out a keyring from his pocket.

Now, thirty years later, somewhere out there in the night shadows of an endless desert, his old friend was dying in a tent that smelled of mildew and camel hair. He wished he could roll back the decades and start again, relive the bonhomie of their university days. Would he make the same choices? he wondered. The same reckless decisions that led him to be cast out from academia and witness more of this marvelous blue dot and the stars beyond than most people in their lifetimes? The same decisions that led him to her?

Rising over a humpback dune, the white outlines of tents glowed in a hazy darkness, the spirit of the night's festivities drifting from the extinguished campfire in the shallow valley. Olivier and Vera climbed down the final slope, the camp serene in its private outpost among the dunes. Everyone had gone to bed, the campfire sloppily abandoned, leaving a mess of dirty bowls and coats and even Moussa's red fez left behind on a crate, which Olivier did note was rather odd. The embers smoldered with cinders kicked loose from the sandpit, faintly glowing under the starlight. The vaulted sky was clear again, the only clouds that remained were those made by fire.

Olivier was bereft. He had hoped Fritz would still be awake, alive and well and laughing by the fire, so he would have the chance to beg his forgiveness for the fallout of their friendship. And yes, of course, for attempting to poison his old friend and convince his wife to run away with him.

"Oh Ollie, I'm sure your cat will turn up," Vera said, noting the worried expression on his face. "Like you said, she knows the desert. She can fend for herself."

Olivier feigned comfort in her words while secretly panicked over the dead or not-quite-dead state of his friend.

"I'll walk you back to your tent," he said.

"I don't think that's a good idea, do you?"

"Well, you know, I want to check in on Fritz. You said he was worried about me."

"He's probably fast asleep by now."

Or expired, Olivier thought.

"Ollie, save it for the morning, okay?"

They said their goodnights. He watched her walk away, her hand slipping from his grip, feeling her energy dissipate in distance between them, desperate for something, anything to make him feel grounded and sane again.

He climbed up the dune on the far side of camp. He hunted along the ridge, his vision greyed out in the darkness, until he came across his Criterion Dynascope. The telescope had fallen over in the sand. He set it upright and secured the tripod, attending to the antique like a nurse caring for an elderly patient. He rubbed the lens clean. He blew out grit from its cylinder. He checked the interior mirrors for any scratches. He tested its magnification and clarity, seeking out Beta Lyrae and its lyrical dance. Roving south, he found Capella in the constellation of Auriga and then Mirfak, pulsing brighter than ever, in a speckled swirl that misted the Persoid belt. Its brother Angol, the devil star, winked too.

Satisfied that the instrument had sustained no lasting damage, Olivier sat down and unstrapped his sandals. He massaged his sore feet, digging his heels into the cool sand. He rolled and smoked a cigarette. He would know soon enough. Vera would find Fritz in their tent, either blissfully asleep or suffering a feverish hell. All was not lost, he convinced himself. Even if Fritz was poisoned, he could still talk his way out of this. He could still do the right thing.

He smoked and thought about the disappointing kiss for which he'd waited a lifetime. He smoked and thought about Tiku. His cat, she'd said. That was laughable. He only adopted her after she began following him up the rooftop of the Port d'Etoile and everywhere else in the arched halls of the dusty riad. She'd been such a loyal friend on so many lonely nights, finding him with his eye in the viewfinder, head in the stars, rubbing against his ankle and purring until he returned to earth. He never deserved her sweetness.

He scratched between his toes, flicking out sand. He spotted the tuna can he'd left out for Tiku. He waved away the flies. He held the tin under the starlight. It was half eaten, the gelatinous cake nibbled at its edges. He listened in the night for her soft meow. And then he heard the screams.

Somewhere down in the camp, somewhere among the canvases haloed by the dying campfire, there came a shrill cry that iced his nerves. It's done then, he thought. He listened for her long sobs. He listened for her desperate wails, her fists pounding the sand. He listened for the others, rousted from their drunken sleep by the mourning call. He smoked, paralyzed by fear, guilt, regret, eying the camp from afar. Strangely there was no movement from the tents, no angry pitchfork mob of Moussa and the astronomers. Nothing but stifled quiet, which was all the more disturbing.

Olivier snuffed out his cigarette. He lingered in the dark until the silence became unbearable. He angled the telescope down from sky and peered in the viewfinder. The camp was strangely quiet. It looked like a ghost town. He scanned the campfire and the tents as if he were a hunter waiting for some unknown predator or prey. Precise, measured increments. A flash of blue cloth crossed his scope, then vanished. Rattled, he chased after it, unable to discover where the flitting specter had gone.

Olivier strapped on his sandals and rose to his feet. He flipped up the collar on his jacket. He was not very adept at heroics. He wished he were a stronger man. Confident, bull-headed. Someone like Fritz. It wasn't the courage to act that frightened him but the clumsiness of his own indecision, that he might stand between life and death with only a split second to react, and flinch, and fail. He breathed deep, said a little prayer of protection to the jester of the universe, and descended the dune into camp.

He was no stranger to fear, but what flooded him then—this vigilance as he moved through the camp like a thief in the all-too-still night—it was something visceral and bewitching. A primal awareness. The stars suddenly shown too bright, his every footfall too loud in the soft sand, his stomach misbehaving from hunger and panic. Every tent he passed was empty, even Fritz and Vera's. There was no sign of anyone anywhere except the vague tremble of a lantern that escaped from the ragged flaps of a worn tent on the far edge of camp.

As he approached, girding the shadows of the dune slopes, it occurred to him that he had not really thought through what he might do if he encountered danger. He had no weapon. He had no plan. But he did have the element of surprise. Whispers murmured out across the sand into the quiet night. People arguing in Arabic and French. He distinctly heard Moussa's voice, the tenor of it unmistakable, like a disappointed teacher scolding dim-witted students. He slinked as close as possible to the tent. He crouched low by the entrance flap. He could hear pieces of the argument. It was political discussion about the exploitation of the Sahara for profit, the autonomy of the tribes, the Moroccan and Algerian authorities who pitted them against each other in a proxy war over the border. The debate was punctuated by anguished moans and muffled screams.

Through the thin gap, opening the flap ever so slightly, he saw them bound. The astronomers were seated cross-legged before their captors like schoolchildren waiting for storytime. Their arms and legs sashed with rope. Their mouths gagged. It was difficult to tell how many kidnappers were inside. Two or three, perhaps another out of sight, arguing with Moussa and Amadou. Youssef was among them, his tall figure in a corner boiling water for tea on a small propane burner.

Allister and Ingrid were quaking in terror. Saul was either still passed out or dead. Olivier couldn't see Vera. However, the giant legs that splayed out into view definitely belonged to Fritz, his feet jerking in their slippers.

"This is a disaster," the nomad in the blue kaftan said in Arabic. "What did you drug them with? This man is sick."

"He's faking," Youssef said, steeping the tea.

"He has a fever," Moussa said. "He needs medical

attention. I highly doubt the rebels would be very happy with how badly you botched this, hmmm? I promise you that, if you release us, we will forget this ever happened."

"You are a disgrace to your people, Moussa. You speak like a foreigner. You think like a foreigner. Trust them, you say. We've trusted their kind over and over and where has it gotten us?"

"And you think more violence is the answer?" he said. "After all the people of the Sahara and Sahel have been through. I am Mali. You don't know me. You don't know what I've done. You don't know what I've seen."

Olivier eavesdropped on their passionate debate. He had never quite heard the argument so clearly articulated. The illegal occupation of their ancestral lands, the corrupt government of Morocco, a puppet, they claimed, for its former colonial masters and the international profiteers who exploited the Sahara for resources while displacing their people and leaving them in poverty. He found himself strangely siding with the kidnappers. As he listened, he became aware of a disquieting presence outside. Someone was snoring like an idle motor behind the tent. He peeked around the side. Lumps in the darkness rose. The camels swung their long necks, shook off their sleep. They gawked at him. The runt of litter bared its buck teeth and snorted.

Olivier froze. The flap whisked open. Hands swept out like a hawk and gripped his shoulders, dragging him inside. The nomad in the blue kaftan threw Olivier onto his knees.

"Sit," he said. "Behave."

In short order, he was tied up with the others.

A touching reunion. The astronomers were glad to see him alive, although somewhat disappointed that he'd been so easily captured. Vera hardly registered his arrival. She sat, numbed and horrified, with her husband's head cradled in her lap, sweat pouring down his tormented face.

The kidnappers were not particularly menacing. They were boys, not much older than teenagers, except for the nomad in the blue kaftan and Youssef whom Olivier presumed was the leader. The kidnappers sipped their tea and considered their options, bickering amongst themselves. They believed the foreigners were either incredibly rich or European royalty. The astrolabe was proof. How else could a foreigner acquire something of such tremendous value? It was 100 years old and had once belonged to a famous sultan, his insignia inscribed on the back.

From what Olivier gathered from the conversation, the kidnappers, after being overjoyed at first by their luck, now found themselves in a quandary with their plans spoiled by Fritz, whom they called "the sick prince." He was an unforeseen burden. He would no doubt die if forced to travel by camel on the twenty-mile journey to the rendezvous point. So, they calmly debated leaving him or putting him out of his misery behind the tent.

The other option was to go back to base camp and steal the foreigners' jeeps, one of the kidnappers argued. The nomad in the blue kaftan dismissed this as too dangerous since the Algerian military patrols were vigilant against motorized vehicles crossing the border, especially in the dead of night. Also, the tribes that warred over the no-man's land would surely attack any vehicle in their territory believing that it was part of a military incursion by the Algerian government. They were stuck with seven hostages and no good options and a man slowly dying in his wife's arms.

"This was not part of plan," the nomad said to Youssef.

Moussa continued to argue with the kidnappers. He told them they were mistaken, that their hostages were tourists and scientists. No one would pay a ransom for their lives.

"He's lying," Olivier said in French. "They are filthy rich."

Moussa whipped his head with a pointed stare.

"We tried to hide it for his safety," Olivier continued. "But yes, this man is royalty. And if anything happens to him, the German government will track you down and kill you all."

"Who is this man? He's not like the others. He dresses like a dog."

"I'm… a doctor," Olivier said.

"Is this true?" Youssef asked.

"Yes," Moussa lied. "He's our resident, ahem, doctor at the hotel."

The nomad in the blue kaftan exchanged glances with the other kidnappers and a few harsh words. There was a short deliberation, which ended abruptly when he knelt down and cut loose the binds. Olivier wiggled his hands and rolled his wrists to tease out the pain.

"Tend to him, doctor," Youssef said. "If he dies, you die."

11.

IN 1979, Olivier had traveled with Dexter to Guatemala on an expedition to the ruins of Tikal and the famed Mayan observatory of Uaxactun. They'd spent seven days trekking through the jungle, skirting scorched rainforests, military tanks, and areas of guerilla combat between government forces and the revolutionaries who were in the midst of a very long and bloody civil war. Dexter, well-trained in firearms from his time in the Black Panthers, had taught Olivier how to properly shoot an AK-47 in preparation for their trip, a rifle which had become the weapon of choice for most Central American insurrections since it was made handily available to both sides of the war by Soviet and U.S. profiteers alike. Dexter and Olivier were so vigilant against the dangers of war—sleeping in shifts while listening to distant gunfire erupt in the night—that they were distracted from other very real indigenous perils of the jungle.

After two whole days exploring the ruins of Tikal, they made it to Uaxactun by dusk and decided to camp in the celestial alignment among the ancient temples erected at the exact vectors of the solstices and equinox. The stars were spectacular, and they drank far too much mezcal than was wise for two dorky scientists in the untamed jungle of a country on the verge of civil collapse. Olivier awoke in the middle of night to the most horrendous screams he'd ever heard in his life. Dexter, with his eyes peeled, clutched his swollen leg. He stared at the red marks where two fangs had punctured the flaky skin of his ankle. The lower half of his body was already paralyzed with the venom's scourge riding up his spinal column and disrupting his nervous system. He struggled to even sputter out the words that might save him.

"Snake… poison." He flailed toward his backpack. "Knife."

Hungover and shaky, with a torch and bowie knife, Olivier followed Dexter's sputtering instructions on how to treat to the wound. Heating the tip of the blade, the precise flaying of the skin around the wound to fully expose the fang incisions, alcohol to clean it thoroughly, and…

"Suck it out?" Olivier said.

"Yes, you son of a bitch," Dexter said. "Do it. Do it now."

Afterward, Olivier bandaged the wound with an antibiotic salve and gauze. Pascal endured a fitful tortuous sleep—from which he didn't fully awake for half a day—while Olivier chain-smoked with the rifle by his side, on guard against whatever might sliver or crawl from the jungle.

With these memories once again fresh in his mind, Olivier crouched beside another gravely ill friend whose spastic moans and rank stench had rendered him human and mortal. Olivier laid a gentle hand on his old friend as Fritz rasped, desperate for a full breath. The kidnappers watched and drank their tea. Olivier listened to the patient's heartbeat—rapid, frantic, and in poor time. Looking up, he met Vera's harried eyes and all the questions they asked, namely what the hell are you doing, and are you trying to get yourself killed? He nodded demonstratively and instructed the kidnappers to fetch a pillow and a damp cloth.

"We need to get him elevated."

The kidnappers roughly propped up his dying friend. Olivier scolded them for their recklessness.

"Watch your tongue, doctor," Youssef said. "Or I'll take it out."

Olivier inspected Fritz's weeping eyes, the eclipsed moons of his pupils. He pressed two fingers on the throbbing veins in his neck, the pulse clumsy. Gently probing, he moved his fingers down the ribcage to the lower abdomen. He applied light pressure on the waist with both hands as the patient cried out and mumbled in tongues. In a moment of inspired theatrics, Olivier paused as if in revelation. He rolled up the cuff of Fritz's pantleg to expose a swollen calf, the muscle and sinew purpled and engorged.

"Ah, yes," Olivier said.

"What is it?" Youssef asked.

Olivier did not respond right away. He focused his concentration on the patient and his performance. He removed Fritz's slippers, searching for the answer he already knew. His foot was jaundiced and bruised, a nasty discoloration that spread out from a small festering wound in his heel.

"Boil more water," Olivier said.

"We don't take orders from you, doctor," Youssef said. "Speak."

Olivier wiped away the encrusted blood and puss, revealing blistered skin round a ragged puncture wound.

"A scorpion," he said.

"I haven't seen a scorpion this far out in the desert for years," the nomad in the blue kaftan said.

"Look at the size of the wound… the reaction. See for yourself."

The nomad bent over and gripped the patient's swollen foot by the ankle. Fritz whelped so loud the tent shook. After a brusque examination, the nomad stood up in disgust. He nodded to Youssef.

"This man will die if we don't get him to a hospital," Olivier said.

"This man will die anyway," the nomad said. "He's too weak."

Olivier tenderly held his old friend's foot. His mouth dry, his mind frantic. He hunched close, the ragged wound glistening on his heel. He had to do this. For Fritz. For Vera. For his own goddamn soul. He closed his eyes and puckered up.

"Blind me, please," Moussa said. "I can't watch this."

"It's okay. I've done this before," Olivier said. "I'm going to suck it out."

"It won't matter," the nomad said. "It's too much in his blood. The whole leg is infected."

"Then at least lend me a knife so I can clean the wound," he said.

The kidnappers deliberated amongst themselves. Whispers, disagreements, a decision. They pulled Olivier away from the patient. Youssef nodded to the youngest of the kidnappers who responded by brandishing a scimitar. The crescent blade gleamed in the lantern light.

"What are you doing?" Olivier asked. The kidnappers said nothing. "What are they doing, Moussa. Tell them to stop."

"They're going to cut off the leg and seal the wound with fire," Moussa replied.

"No, there's another way. I have medicine. Tell them I have medicine."

Moussa studied him with a confused and curious look. "What medicine?"

"Antivenom," he said. "In my doctor's kit."

Moussa relayed the message. There was a hushed discussion among the kidnappers.

"Okay, let's go," the nomad in the blue kaftan said, his smile wide and sharp. Moussa said something quick to Olivier, in broken Dutch, what sounded like nonsense… waffle in the hut? He said it twice and with such urgency that Olivier understood it as a warning. The nomad slung a rifle on his shoulder. He grabbed Olivier by the jacket and shoved him out of the tent.

*

THE night felt cooler on the forced march through camp. The nomad kept one hand clasped on Olivier's neck like a camel, the other on the rifle, prodding him along with stiff jabs. Olivier could hardly control his shivering. The chill made his skin feel reptilian, the ying-yang coin rattled on his chest with every gust of wind, the sand like crushed ice underneath his sandals. He still had no plan, only a trajectory and some 30 meters to figure out what he'd do once they reached their destination. Passing the campfire, he conspired to turn and shove the nomad into the hot embers at just the right moment. While considering the pros and cons, he missed his chance.

The nomad pressed the rifle barrel into his backside. "Where?"

Olivier gestured toward the dune on the far side of camp. The nomad grunted under his breath and shoved him with the rifle. Waffle in the hut? The cryptic message circled through Olivier's mind. What was Moussa trying to tell him? Was it a metaphor? Was he cursing at him? He remembered once at breakfast during his first month at Port d'Etoile when Olivier, homesick, had convinced Madame Habib to make him some Belgian waffles. Moussa had ridiculed him, saying it looked like someone had stepped on his crêpes. Waffle in the hut?

Now was his opportunity, he thought, as they left the outskirts of camp and began their ascent, his telescope visible on the summit. All he needed to do was turn and push him down. But he could barely manage to hike the dune, his sandals sinking deep in avalanches of sand. He glanced over his shoulder, seized by vertigo under the spinning stars. The nomad observed him with his rifle sighted, climbing with such ease it seemed as if he were floating up the slope.

At last, Olivier reached the peak and slowly tread toward the telescope. He didn't need to look to know the nomad was there. He could feel his presence behind him. He choked down his fear. The rucksack was where he'd left it beside the telescope. His beloved Criterion Dynascope. Was it big enough? Could he do it? Its thick metal cylinder would certainly crack a bone. The telescope had been gifted to him by his grandfather when he left to study at the Sorbonne. Was this the best plan? It was an antique. One of a kind. Sentimental, yes, but also arguably valuable.

"What are you waiting for?" the nomad said. "Grab it."

Olivier began rummaging through his rucksack. Time, he needed time to think. He unrolled the antivenom from the sock in which he'd hidden it in the bag. With a quick sleight of hand, he slipped the bottle in his pocket and continued to search. The nomad stood guard, growing bored or suspicious, he couldn't tell which. Olivier wanted to aggravate his captor. He wanted him to come within striking distance and then, yes then, he would have to act. If only he had a real weapon. Then it dawned on him. Moussa's cryptic message. Waffe, not waffle. Moussa wasn't speaking Dutch. He has trying to speak German, confusing the "v" annunciation of the "w". Waffe im hut… weapon in the hat.

"Drats, my med kit is not here," Olivier said, closing the rucksack. "Ah, I know. It's by the campfire."

He gave the nomad a long-winded explanation about how he must have left his kit there after he'd given one of the astronomer's some medicine for stomach cramps.

"You're lying." the nomad said.

"I'm not lying. I told you—"

"Show me what's in your pocket."

"There's nothing in my pocket."

"Show it."

"There's nothing."

"You're lying. I've lived in the desert all my life. I've dealt with your kind, foreigners who lie and lie and lie and make promises only to break them when it serves their interests. You think you are smarter than me because you live in your head and not in your hands. But I know. I know when a man is lying to me."

"Alright, yes, fine, I did find a small bottle of anesthetic in case we need to operate."

"You're still lying. Why are you lying?"

"I swear to you—"

"You're not a doctor."

The strength and speed of his movements surprised Olivier, how light the telescope felt compared to the velocity of his rage as he grabbed the telescope and swung, hitting the nomad straight in the midriff with enough force to send him buckling to the sand.

Sliding, stumbling down the slope, Olivier rushed toward the campfire with the repetition of Moussa's words in his head—waffe im hut… weapon in the hat. On a crate by the smoldering embers, he spotted Moussa's red fez. He snatched the hat and ran off, seeking cover behind a nearby tent as the first gunshots rang out. There was a hard bulge inside the brim. He ripped the seam and slipped out a stone blade from its hiding place—a slim Tuareg dagger with an emerald in its hilt.

He had little time to admire its craftsmanship. The

nomad swooped from the darkness like a bird of prey with his full weight upon him, shoving his face into the desert. Olivier struggled to breathe, choking on cold grains of sand, his brain deprived of oxygen. Panic subsided with a slow suspension of time. This is it, he thought. This is what? This is the moment I die. This is how I die. This is where it ends. The thought began to really bother him. He wrenched back for air. The nomad slammed his head into the sand again. It reminded him of all the times he was teased for his thick glasses and goofy haircut, all the times the schoolyard bullies would shove his face in the playground dirt and order him to eat worms. He'd always believed that if he ever met those bullies again, he'd have the last laugh, that his intellect would prevail over their brutality. Gasping for air with the darkness taking hold, he realized he was wrong. You are no longer that frightened kid, he told himself. You are a man about to die in the desert if you don't stop acting like a goddamn child.

He bucked against the indominable weight, then bucked again and again until he freed his arm, jabbing backward. He felt the stone blade sink through the cloth and absorb deep into the flesh. The nomad let out a gurgling scream. His weight fell off him. Olivier lifted his bruised face, cold air filling his lungs. The nomad knelt in a pool of wet sand. He clutched his blue kaftan, attempting to dam the flood from his abdomen. Whatever organ the dagger had pierced, blood was rushing out of him faster than he could hold it in. The nomad fumbled for his rifle and collapsed.

✳

ONCE the shock wore off, a minute, maybe more, time slow and curious, Olivier rubbed his caked eyes and blinked until the starlight gleamed again. He steadied his breathing and gathered himself, wiping blood off the Tuareg dagger. He stood over the nomad in the blue kaftan passed out from blood loss. He did not think. He did not deliberate on the possible options and outcomes. He only acted. He stripped off the nomad's headscarf and bound it around his own head. He picked up the rifle and slung it over his shoulder. He then turned toward the ragged tent at the far edge of camp. The bell tolled in his mind, loud and clear, echoing out over the dunes.

Olivier stalked through camp with the rifle gripped like a rookie soldier. He was not afraid anymore. His tremors were involuntary, an aftereffect of shock. The baby-faced kidnappers came out from the tent, no doubt summoned by the disturbing sounds that had traveled across the dune gulley. At first and second glance, they were thrown off-guard by the shadowy figure in the blue headscarf. Olivier rocketed off gunshots into the stars above their heads. They scrambled onto their camels, yelling and cursing, bullets chasing after them as they rode off into the night.

Olivier wrenched hard on the rifle winch and reloaded. There was no further movement from the tent, although he could faintly hear delirious moaning inside. He steeled himself and whipped open the flap.

Youssef sat on a stool with the scimitar, finishing his cup of tea. Fritz was propped up in front of him like a ghastly mannequin. The old man sipped his tea, more annoyed than frightened by the bumbling foreigner with a rifle unsteady in his grip.

"Sit. We talk," he said. "Maybe we come to agreement."

Olivier leveled the rifle at the old man. "Let them go."

Youssef set down his teacup, and in the same motion, swept up and throttled Fritz with his forearm. He drew the crescent blade to his jugular. "You move. He dies."

"He dies. You die," Olivier said.

"I die. He dies."

"How about none of us die?" Moussa said. "And we just go home?"

Fritz's eyes flexed wide, forehead greased with sweat, Adam's apple quivering under the curved blade. Vera thrashed in her binds and threw herself to the sand. She screamed into her gag, crawling toward Youssef. Olivier stepped out in front of her, his rifle trained on the old man, his hip cocked so Vera could see the stone dagger in his belt.

Youssef muttered something aside in Arabic to Moussa. Olivier asked him what he'd said.

"He said your idiot doctor is going to let the prince die because he thinks he's a hero," Moussa said. "He said the doctor must not like him much to let him suffer such a terrible death."

Olivier held firm to his stoic resolve and the rifle while suffering a torrent of guilt and regret.

"He's no prince," he said. "But he is a good man who doesn't deserve this. He's my oldest friend. My best friend."

Fritz erupted with a bellyful of laughter, painful and phlegmy.

"Good one, Ollie!" he said, croaking out the words.

"Is that why you poisoned me, huh? Like friends do, right? A lizard… I should've known. What a farce."

"Fritz, you're delirious, please. Save your strength."

"Be done with it, Ollie," he said. "All for love. Do it, straight to the heart and clean on through."

Fritz convulsed with guffaws. Youssef struggled to keep his hostage upright, cautious of the curved blade on their throat.

Olivier's finger trembled on the trigger. He could chance the shot. And what were his chances at such a close range? He began to run the math—the distance, kickback, variances in alignment—when he felt something chew at his waist. Glancing quickly, he spied Vera with the dagger between her teeth. She huddled into her knees, trying to saw at her binds.

"Let him go," Ollie said to Youssef. "Then we talk."

Youssef tightened his hold on the hostage, disturbed by a subtle commotion in the tent.

"Shoot, Ollie," Fritz said. "Stop being such a dussledork."

Olivier could feel the moment approaching, the wave of destiny bound to crash. He could see it crest in the mounting anxiety from Youssef. He stilled his racing thoughts and calculations. He focused on the moment. He readied himself for the inevitable, watching panic sweep the old man's face as Vera's binds fell from her wrists. Youssef would falter. He would make a mistake. Olivier swore he would not hesitate. Not this time. Not ever again.

"Ah, you can't, huh?" Fritz said. "Not facing me like a man, eye to eye? Would you rather I pretend to be unconscious so you can murder me in my sleep?"

Olivier's vision blurred. Fritz was a Baroque painting of aristocratic decay. Were these schoolyard taunts or a plea for mercy? His grip tightened. Youssef's eyes darted side to side. Then came an unsettling rustle from somewhere behind him, a light breeze from outside. Shadows climbed the canvas walls, toying with his imagination. His nerves electrified. The nomad in the blue kaftan, risen from the dead, he thought. The shadow moved swift, growing bigger, taking shape until it loomed like a giant in the lantern light—monstrous, hunch-backed, and furry.

Youssef sprung up from the stool with his scimitar, dropping Fritz's huge body to the sand. The tabby cat dodged his swinging sword. She dashed away in an erratic sprint, knocking over the lantern and spilling flaming oil across the sand. In that split second, Olivier took aim at the old man's chest. He did not hesitate. The gunshot thundered.

It would have been a precise and deadly shot. Unfortunately, at that exact moment, Moussa, who had likewise been waiting for this opportunity, acted without hesitation as well, leaping forward to tackle Youssef and catching the bullet in his hip.

Smoke and heat filled the tent as flames ate the canvas walls. Vera cut Saul and Amadou loose from their binds, Fritz cursed Olivier for being a coward, Moussa cursed Olivier for being a lousy shot, and Olivier scanned the smoky haze with his rifle for the kidnapper who'd somehow disappeared. The astronomers fled in a panic, dragging the wounded out into the open air.

The stars swirled over the desert, spinning out of control. The camels were all gone except for the runt with the mohawk. Olivier raced up a dune and sighted his rifle. There, some hundred meters off, he could faintly spy Youssef, camel bound and trotting off into the no man's land. Olivier fired again and again until it clicked empty, hitting nothing but space and the darkness in between.

The carousel of stars slowed but his heart still thundered. He felt a familiar scratching at his ankles. He slung the rifle over his shoulder and hunched down beside Tiku.

"Quite pleased with yourself, aren't you?" he said, stroking her fur. "Yes, you did well, you little troublemaker."

Olivier caressed her ears. Tiku nuzzled her face into his sore hands, her nose wet and whiskers ticklish. He scooped Tiku into his arms, thunder settling in his chest, overpowered by her softness.

*

BY the time Olivier trundled down from the dune with his cat, there was a wartime triage for the wounded, illuminated by the ragged tent in flames. Allister tended to Moussa, helping him clot the bullet hole in his hip and feeding him wine for the pain. Amadou and Saul saddled the runt camel on a mission to fetch the jeeps at base camp. Vera sat with the body of her husband in the sand. Olivier slowed when he noticed how she held his lolling head. She said nothing when he asked her questions. She was quaking so hard he felt capsized in the wake of her despair.

Olivier crouched beside her. He laid a hand on

Fritz's chest. The ribcage rose and fell. The light in his old friend's eyes was dim, however the pupils tracked movement. Olivier reached inside his pocket and pulled out the bottle of antivenom. He instructed Vera to purse open his lips.

"What is that?" she asked.

"Medicine." He took hold of her hand and squeezed. "It's going to be okay."

There was little warmth in her touch. No comfort, no tingling electricity between them. Stroking her husband's hair, Vera stared at Olivier obliquely. He dismissed her oddness as shock, although he couldn't shake the ingratitude of it. Such coldness, such indifference after he'd single-handedly saved them all and possibly killed a man in the process. He glanced over by the campfire. There was no sign of the nomad in the blue kaftan.

"What kind of medicine, Ollie?"

"Antivenom," he said, distracted. "Scorpion antivenom."

He lifted the bottle to his friend's blistered lips and poured it down his throat. "Come on, swallow. There you go, that's it, that's right."

Fritz gurgled on the viscous liquid.

"Scorpion antivenom," Vera repeated to herself. "Like for giant black scorpions?"

"Yes, that's right. Tip his chin up? We're almost done," Olivier said as the last drops of antivenom oozed from the bottle onto the patient's tongue. Fritz's breathing steadied. His legs spasmed. He muttered Vera's name, over and over. She hushed and held him until his body calmed and his moans lulled.

A broad smile stretched across Vera's face, beaming at Olivier with what felt like gratitude. Maybe even admiration? His heart swelled with love for her. Like in the storybooks, he had vanquished the conspiring forces of evil and protected the innocent from certain doom. He had proven himself a man of courage, a man of valor, a hero.

"You did this," she said.

"Yes, yes I did," Olivier said with pride.

Her gentle face turned to stone. "You poisoned him."

"No, of course not."

"Tell me it isn't true, Ollie."

Olivier rose from the sand. "We should let him sleep. You should rest too. It will be a couple hours before they return with jeeps. It's been a terrible night."

"Look at me," she demanded. He'd never seen her so angry. The fury seemed to birth new stars in her nebulous eyes. He was so rattled that he hardly registered the Tuareg dagger in her fist.

"You did this, you jackass. The black scorpion in the jar. I can't believe you did this."

"Calm down, please. I don't know what you are talking about."

"You think you are so clever, don't you? My god, Ollie. What were you thinking? You tried to murder him. Why? For some petty grudge?"

"Vera, seriously. Let's—"

"Answer me."

Olivier turned away. He clutched his chest and felt himself start to hyperventilate. He could not suffer the paring of her virulent stare, stripping him of his costume until the naked truth remained—that he was just a scared little boy with a gun playing soldier in the desert of a foreign land.

"Answer me, Ollie. Why?"

He felt so feeble then, so vulnerable. He could never hide anything from her. She'd always seen through his clever lies. If he stayed any longer, he would be undone.

"You're tired. Get some sleep," he said and walked away.

All would be forgotten by morning, he reasoned, once they were far away from this dreadful place. The disaster of their adventure in the Sahara a foggy nightmare, the details of which were better left in obscurity. He reassured himself with these thoughts, gazing up at the seraphic night sky over the Sahara. And then he heard her scream, lurching from the sand, her body falling upon him as the dagger's tip pierced deep between his shoulder blades with mind-numbing pain.

12.

THERE was nothing but the vacuum of space and his disembodied self among the stars. Peaceful, eternal, motionless. He was stationary, frozen among the starlight. He had no body, only roving telescopic eyes in the void. Hours of silence. Hours of stillness. No movement beyond the stars like hearts ablaze in the nothingness. They dimmed, they brightened, they pulsed. They extinguished in a magic trick, a wink into oblivion, then reflamed like a cough from a cosmic bellows. Ever so faintly, they began to ring. He dreaded this, every time, how the stars twinkled with a high-pitched frequency, louder and louder until he became acutely aware of his body and the horrible pain.

Olivier was foisted from his slumber by the infuriating jingle in his room. Tiku was curled on his bed, undisturbed by the obnoxious bell or the commotion in the hall—nurses shouting in French, the bustle of feet in the riad halls. He lifted himself up momentarily and collapsed again, overpowered by the searing pain that enflamed his back, the stitches stretched taut under the gauze.

In his drug-induced haze, it felt like it had been months since their nightmare in the desert. He remembered little of their escape except the thunderous shaking and harrowing roar of the jeeps on their midnight ride over the dunes. He did however remember their arrival at dawn to the gates of the Port d'Etoile, how the color drained from Karl's face when the wounded were loaded out of the jeeps. He had called in a doctor from Zagora who rushed to the scene with several nurses, medical equipment, and morphine, transforming the riad into a makeshift clinic.

Madame Habib visited twice a day with meals. No one else came to see him, aside from a nurse who would check his progress and inject him with a sedative for another night suspended in the dreamy cosmos. Thankfully Madame Habib usually brought some gossip in the morning with his breakfast. Moussa was expected to make a full recovery after the doctor had successfully extracted the bullet lodged in his hip. Fritz, on the other hand, had yet to regain consciousness. The doctor had been able to stabilize his condition and administer a series of transfusions that they hoped would improve his chances. Black scorpion venom is very deadly, she asserted, and his system need time to recover from the shock. Karl had told the staff that Olivier was not to leave his room under any circumstances until further notice.

"Am I under arrest?" he asked.

"Eat your breakfast, Ollie," she said. "I'm sure Karl will visit when he's ready."

The perfectly hard-boiled eggs that she delivered every morning with a side of toast and snippets of gossip were of little comfort to him as he stewed in his misery and guilt. Every day he waited for a knock, a letter, a word, for some messenger of forgiveness. Occasionally he would amble out into the halls, but he never ventured too far from his chambers. He would listen out on the mezzanine for her voice in the birdsong rising up from the canaries in their cages that hung in the grand hall. Sometimes he imagined he heard it, her sweet voice in the echo, feeling an involuntary flutter in his chest, which inevitably triggered shallow breaths and the fiery sting of his three-inch stab wound.

After a week of this limbo, there came a knock on his door in the late afternoon from an unexpected visitor. Moussa, in his double-breasted waistcoat, red fez rakish on his head, limped to his bedside aided by a wooden cane. A messenger finally. An executioner, more like it, Olivier thought. However, Moussa showed none of his usual malice. He settled himself in a chair by the bedside and crossed his legs, even though it obviously pained him to do so.

"Hello, Ollie," he said. "Feeling better?"

"Worse, better, what's the difference?" Olivier said. "What do you want, Moussa? Are you here to gloat?"

"If you're going to be crabby, I'll leave."

"Fine, go."

"Fine, be that way." Moussa struggled to rise from the chair and fumbled, losing his balance and almost spilling on the floor. Olivier sprang up from his bed and helped steady him. The invalids both resettled again opposite each other, exhausted and sore from their private agonies.

"I'm sorry—"

"For shooting me or for being a literal pain in the ass?"

"Both," Olivier said. "Stay a moment. Karl sent you?"

"I came on my own."

Moussa relayed the news as told to him by Karl. There was an investigation underway, a private affair for now, however Karl had alerted the authorities to the desert safari outfit through which they had booked the guides. When questioned over the phone, the tour company, Glorious Magic Desert Dreams, had denied any culpability, pointing to a fine print clause in the contract regarding "dangers of the desert" that absolved them as any third-party liability for the conduct of the guides. The phone number for Glorious Magic Desert Dreams had been disconnected shortly thereafter.

Karl had been interviewing the astronomers, trying to disentangle what happened out in the Sahara. There were several versions of the story, some more outlandish than others, some hewing closer to the truth. In the patchwork tale, there was a subtle insinuation that Olivier might have been an accomplice in the kidnapping.

"That's absurd!" Olivier said.

"You know Karl," Moussa said. "He's paranoid when it comes to business. He never trusts my count, checks the drawer every night, questions the ledgers. He thinks this is all part of some grand conspiracy. Nobody wanted him to build the Port d'Etoile and the authorities haven't warmed to him over the years. It doesn't help that Vera has admitted to stabbing you, but she won't tell anyone why."

"So why doesn't he come talk to me himself?"

"He's waiting to hear Fritz's side of the story."

Moussa described his old friend's miraculous recovery, how he'd surfaced a few days prior after two weeks in a near-vegetative state. The infected wound had healed, the swelling and jaundice in his leg subsided. His breathing was heavy and rattled but his oxygen levels were on the rise and his heart had steadied its pace. The poison, it seemed, had left him with no permanent nerve damage except for spotted bruising from burst blood vessels.

"He's awake, though obviously still delirious. He keeps asking for you like a child and alternately cursing your name."

"Well, I'd like to see him."

"Neither Karl nor the doctors would allow that." Moussa leaned forward in his chair. "How do I explain this to you? You're in great danger. I've seen Karl like this before. I fear that he's looking for a scapegoat for what happened… and you, my friend, are it."

Olivier sat upright and called Tiku over to his lap. She obliged and nestled there. He petted her to calm his nerves.

"So I'm doomed to be the sacrificial lamb."

"Ollie, you may be an extraordinary screw-up, but I owe you my life," Moussa said. "You saved the lives of all those arrogant twits, whether or not they realize it. Kidnappings of tourists in the desert never end well. Nor the fate of foreigners that end up in our jails."

"He wouldn't."

"Don't underestimate his anger."

"What should I do?"

"Gather your things and leave tonight."

"You'd love that, wouldn't you?" Olivier laughed. "What kind of trick is this?"

Moussa bowed his head, unclasping a chain from his neck. He passed over a Tuareg necklace. The amulet was shaped like a shield, finely etched with ornate geometric lines and inlaid with a black agate gemstone at its center surrounded by four embossed triangles like compass points. Olivier measured the weight of the amulet in his palm. This wasn't any cheap souk trinket. It was made of copper, brass, silver.

"Trying to buy me off? It won't work, Moussa. You'll see, I'll prove my innocence."

"That amulet has been in my family for generations, Ollie. Consider it a debt paid." Moussa rose from the chair with the help of his cane. "May it protect you on your journey, wherever you may go."

*

AFTER hours of ruminating over Moussa's warning—litigating his innocence against an imaginary judge and jury, again and again—Olivier packed up his meager belongings in the suitcase with which he had arrived in the desert nine years ago. Around midnight, he climbed up to the roof one last time and said goodbye to the glorious stars over the Port d'Etoile, resisting the temptation to smash the lenses in every telescope up there. Once he'd made his peace, he slipped out through the riad halls with his suitcase. He wanted so desperately to knock on every guest room until he found her. He didn't care about Karl. He respected that Fritz would probably hate him for the rest of his life. But Vera… it felt like someone had stolen his heart and replaced it a heavy lump of lead, the weight of which he carried step by step down the stairs and out into the night.

No one saw him. Moussa was conspicuously absent from his post at the front desk. The canaries didn't even stir to herald his departure. His only witness was Tiku who scurried after him as soon as he pushed open the arched doors into the portico courtyard and up the gravel path toward the iron gates. He exhausted himself arguing with the stubborn kitten, telling her to go, that she would be happier if she stayed at the riad. He walked out through the gates. The tabby cat followed.

Together they walked for hours under the stars along the winding road through the Tinfu dunes. Tiku didn't seem to mind the journey. When she eventually became too tired to continue, she refused to let him walk off and abandon her. She meowed until he lifted her onto his shoulders so she could be carried like a tiny furry queen.

The next morning, after a short rest in the dunes wrapped in a blanket, they made it to highway N9 and began heading toward Zagora, some 30 km northwest. From there, with any luck, they could catch the bus to Ouarzazate, bastion of modern civilization in the Draa Valley, a small city that operated as a movie town where production companies from around the world shot films and television shows out on elaborate stage sets in the desert.

And then? Who knows? He could go anywhere. He imagined what it would feel like to reach the other side of the Atlas Mountains, free from this godforsaken desert forever. The sun was so hot and blinding, the road searing through his cheap rubber soles, that he traded his sandals for boots and stripped down to a t-shirt. He wrapped his head in a scarf, remembering the way Vera had threaded and tucked the stray locks of his bushy hair behind his ears in the Sahara.

The scar between his shoulder blades itched, his heart lurched, the ying-yang coin burned against his chest. He removed the medallion. He pulled out the Taureg amulet that Moussa had given him. He clasped the chain around his neck, its stone cool and calming. He held the yin-yang medallion in his palm one last time. The Tao that can be told is not the eternal Tao, he reminded himself, tossing it into the dunes.

As they continued along the side of the highway road, Olivier considered sticking out his thumb to hitch a ride. Since only foreigners hitchhiked in Morocco, this seemed unwise. A car or truck would pass every once in a while. More often, they came across cloaked merchants with their wares, donkey carts, women with baskets and jugs, schoolchildren holding each other's hands on the arduous journey by foot between the tiny villages of sandstone houses that dotted the road like broken clay pottery scattered by a giant.

By the afternoon of the second day, they'd traveled less than 15 kilometers, frequently resting, the two of them eating tuna from the tin and greedily drinking water until there was none left in his canteen. Then he switched to his tallboy beers, along with a rolled cigarette, mindful of the traffic that swerved around him as his straight line forward began to bend.

By dusk, he was so drunk and depressed that Tiku

was the one leading the way, the tabby cat stopping every few yards, meowing as she waited for him to catch up. Olivier dragged his heels through chunks of broken tar. He stuck his thumb out, hoping someone would either stop or knock him dead. The sky darkened, permeated with stars. He was getting ready to give up and bunk off in the dunes when he heard a deep rumble. He gathered Tiku into his arms and stepped out of the way. An RV barreled down the road, careening past them. It abruptly braked, erupting a cloud of dust and tar that scattered, blowing backward. Olivier wiped the grit from his face. He stared at the boxy automobile idling in the twilight, not entirely convinced that it wasn't a mirage. Tiku clung to his chest, her furry head craned, frightened but curious. They went to investigate.

As they approached, the passenger door swung open. And there she stood on the short stairs with her arms crossed. She glared down with a fragile anger, tender and raw. Olivier looked up at her with Tiku in his arms—two strays, one drunk, the other very hungry and sleepy. He squinted into the cockpit of the RV, looking for any knives, clubs, or cudgels that might be close at hand. He could see the curve of Fritz's head in the driver's seat.

"So… are you coming or what?" Vera asked.

Olivier ascended the stairs, wonky and uncertain in his step. She took his luggage and stowed it away in the back, disappearing into the interior. Tiku squirmed out of his arms and followed her behind the curtain. Olivier waited in disbelief. He expected at any moment for Vera to return and boot him down the stairs, bouncing out into the desert like tumbleweed.

Fritz breathed unevenly in the driver's seat, his huge hands gripped on the wheel. His face was blotched with bruises, his eyes bloodshot and glassy.

"Should you be driving?" Olivier asked.

"Left leg is lame, the other is fine," he said. "Should you really be offering your unsolicited opinions right now?"

"Fritz—"

"Thank her," he said. "I would have run you over."

Fritz wiped his eyes dry as Vera came out from the curtain. She sat down in the center seat between them. She instructed Olivier to buckle up. He obeyed. Fritz revved the engine and shifted into gear. The RV lurched onto the highway road, steadily gaining speed.

The twilight dimmed into perfect dark with swathes of stars and nebula visible over the Draa Valley through the windshield. Olivier sunk into his seat. His stomach woozy, his mind blank, his heart sore. Fritz was angrily shaking, gunning the engine. Vera pried his trembling fingers from the wheel and squeezed his hand. She then reached out to Olivier with her other hand and did the same.

They stared out the window together, mesmerized by the road ahead cutting through the lonely desert, the night sky percolating with the maddening starlight and its radiant mystery, accelerating toward the billion points of light and their infinite possibilities.

THE END

ACKNOWLEDGEMENTS

Thank you to the constellation of brilliant kind people who made this book possible. James Reich, editor and publisher extraordinaire, for taking a chance on this novella. The Queens University brigade – Jenny Maattala, Mara Aguilar Egan, and Alex Kuzio for late nights of red wine, cigarettes, and philosophy under the stars. Elissa Schappell for her fiery counsel, wisdom, and wit. Patrick Ryan, Ashley Warlick, Jonathan Dee, Natashia Deon, Jasmin Darznik, and Fred Leebron for their advocacy and mentorship. Myla Goldberg for her merciless notes. Rebecca Bonnar, queen of banter, for her encouragement, support, and pragmatic advice inside & outside the writing life. Sasha Waintraub for her keen eye, humor, and perennial optimism. Simona Blat and the Black Spring Books crowd for creating a literary sanctuary for wayward poets & novelists. My family, friends, and of course, the starry-eyed wonderer Charlotte Royer who enlisted me on many wild adventures over the years, most notably a journey deep into the Moroccan desert in search of the perfect night sky.

DW ARDERN

DW Ardern is a novelist, comic, and screenwriter living in Brooklyn, NY with a mischievous rabbit named Hazel and too many books. His stories have appeared in *The Fourth River*, *Vestal Review*, *Fictive Dream*, *Jabberwock Review*, *Oyster River Pages*, and *The Offbeat* among others. He is the founding editor of *EXCERPT*, a lit art magazine for emerging fiction writers, and holds an MFA in Fiction & Screenwriting from Queens University of Charlotte.